TAILORED FOR HER PRINCE

JAYNE KINGSLEY

BLUEBERRY LANE
PUBLISHING

ALSO BY JAYNE KINGSLEY

ANTHOLOGIES

April Showers: A Seasonal Romance Anthology

Christmas on Hope Street: A Cathedral Springs Christmas Anthology

STAND ALONE

Loving Lucas

THE STENISH ROYALS

#1 Tailored for Her Prince (February 6 2020)

#2 A Convenient Playboy Prince (April 16 2020)

#3 Guarding His Runaway Princess (Coming June 2020)

*For my upcoming famous and fabulous gals & fictional fairies -
you keep me writing.*

1

———

*I*f the prince kept moving, Eva would end up measuring more than just his inseam.

Mentally rolling her eyes, she jotted down an adjustment before taking a step back to assess the slim line of the pants.

"I think they are too long." His cheeky tone interrupted her thoughts as he shifted his right leg, kicking out the hem. *Was he making fun?* She flicked a glance at the clock—half an hour of miniscule changes, yet the suit still evaded perfection to her trained eye.

Plucking a dress pin from between her lips, she bent to adjust the right leg hem a fraction. Standing again, Eva checked her previous fit notes. The jacket lapels needed to be slimmed down and the cuff buttons should be contrasting. Noir silk perhaps, to match the Armani shirt the prince had brought to the fitting. Perfection was Eva's middle name, and she had to get this outfit right. The company, and Gramps, were counting on her.

"You know I was only joking, right?" Felix said.

Eva returned Prince Felix's grin with a nod. After one

appointment, a few things were clear to Eva. The prince was a born flirt, with a body made to drive women to distraction. Broad shoulders held the fine wool Eva draped across them beautifully.

They did nothing for Eva.

Tapping a blossom pink fingernail to her mouth, she took a slow walk around the form before her, analysing every seam, every stretch of fabric. He'd selected the silver-grey superfine and Eva approved. The tone was brought to life by his suntanned skin and ash blonde hair. With the black silk shirt, and slim tie, he'd be a shoo-in for a James Bond lookalike, which was the style of suit he'd asked for. God knew why.

"You know, Eva, if I may call you that... you're hard to figure out."

"Why's that, Your Highness?"

"Felix, please." The prince captured her hand, bringing her focus to him. The move gave her pause, uneasiness creeping into her stomach at the unwanted touch. "I'm not your prince, after all. Tell me about yourself?"

"What would you like to know, Your Highness?" Eva wasn't trying to be evasive, but she couldn't fathom what he wanted to hear. "I'm a Savile Row Tailor, my grandfather is Ernesto James. He taught me everything I know."

Her Gramps was one of the best in the business, his reputation impeccable. Eva made sure every piece of work she did lived up to that standard. Fitting for a prince from the small Northern European country of Stenaco might be a first but she planned to act just as she did with every other client. Cordial, polite and extremely professional.

"I see I'm not going to win the battle of name etiquette, am I? Something to work on next time, perhaps." The prince's left eyebrow rose as his eyes searched Eva's.

Keeping her expression carefully neutral, Eva said nothing.

"You're tougher than you look, Miss James."

"You may call me Eva, Your Highness."

"Finally, she consents to something. Tell me what you do when you're not tailoring to the high and mighty? Do you have hobbies? A boyfriend? Young children dressed in splendidly made clothes?"

The right corner of Eva's lips lifted. "No, Your Highness, no children or significant other. I have a small group of close friends from my time at design school, and in my spare time, I read." Removing her hand, Eva moved over to her sewing bench to make a few notes on the order.

"See? Now that wasn't so hard, was it?" The twinkle was back in his eyes.

"Of course not, Your Highness." Eva double checked the notes she'd written. Lapels, finish lining, additional inside pocket, buttons—it was all there. "I believe I have everything required. Thank you for coming in. I'll finish these today and have them delivered first thing tomorrow." Bowing her head slightly, Eva struggled to remember if she should curtsy or not before leaving the room. She'd never fitted royalty and wasn't sure on the protocol. Would the rules for Stenaco even be the same as they were in England?

Get a grip, Eva. Stop causing yourself undue stress and over-thinking things.

The request to see Prince Felix of Stenaco had only arrived three days prior. Eva had done some shuffling, knowing a new client, one with royal lineage, could be the difference she needed to ensure her gramps' business didn't falter. The work would see her hand-stitching until three a.m. again, but it would be worth it. Every stitch, every line perfectly crafted by hand, every minute detail would put her one step closer to success.

The prince's mouth lifted in a small quirk. *Damn.* She guessed her awkwardness had shown.

"One more moment of your time, Eva, if you don't mind." The prince's words didn't offer refusal as an option.

Eva hooked her hands together, standing ramrod straight. *Oh God. Please don't ask me on a date.*

He shrugged out of the partially sewn pieces of jacket. Stepping down from the fit dais, he moved leisurely to hang the fabric on the mannequin guarding the corner of the room. Eva tensed, waiting for him to speak his request.

"How would you feel about taking a royal appointment? We have tailors in Stenaco, but I'm looking for someone ... different. After today, I know I don't need to see more of what you produce to know you're that person."

Eva opened her mouth to reply, but no words formed. She'd been expecting a proposition, but not a work-related one. *Thank goodness!* Her shoulders sagged with relief that she wouldn't have to navigate a tactful decline. The tightness in her chest eased, freeing her mind and mouth. Work-related offers she could handle.

"Your Highness, if I may speak plainly, your offer comes as a shock." Eva chose her words carefully, widening her eyes to prove her point and gain herself a little thinking time. She averted her gaze as the prince changed back into his own clothes. He obviously felt no shame swanning around half-naked before a woman he'd only met twice.

Taking a deep breath, Eva exhaled slowly, running her hands along the crisp tucks of her tailored indigo pants. She'd never aspired to be anything other than a tailor, to keep the business alive in an ever-dying industry. Sure, she had dreams, but they were hidden. Locked away in her design books.

Besides, she couldn't leave her gramps, not when he was sick. She was needed here to keep the flailing business ticking over. Of course ... a royal appointment would be amazing, maybe even a significant enough income to cover their expenses until she could work out a way to increase business, but what would her gramps do without her here? She couldn't possibly even consider this request, could she?

Prince Felix lifted her chin with a single finger, his slate-blue eyes capturing hers. She swallowed, his proximity a little unnerving. Something about his eyes were familiar, reminding her of ... *no don't go there Eva.*

"Just have a think on it," Felix murmured. "I'll have my assistant drop over the offer later today."

The door whooshed open behind her.

"For God's sake, Felix, do you have to paw at every unsuspecting female you meet? We're late." The voice slammed into her present like it was yesterday. Had she conjured him?

Ignoring the goosebumps that rippled along her bare arms, she craned her neck over her shoulder. Her brain disconnected from the rest of her body, shock ripping through every synapse.

Five years weren't enough to erase the thoughts and feelings that tumbled into her soul when she locked eyes with the man who stood commanding the doorway of her fitting room.

"Henrik." His name was a whisper on her breath.

Eva's shock turned to confusion at the sight of two burly, suit clad men flanking Henrik. They looked a lot like bodyguards.

"Nothing wrong with appreciating beauty when one

finds it, brother dear. Miss Eva James is a fine talent. Her hands create magic. Your own style could use updating; perhaps you should try her wares."

Wait, brother? *Henrik is Felix's brother... He's royalty?* Her knees sagged as question after question tumbled through her mind. *Why hadn't he told her he was royalty? Was that why he disappeared? Was he ordered away? Stop!* She needed to focus.

Henrik's azure gaze bore deep into her own. Her body turned of its own accord as his measured gait drew to a standstill before her.

"Miss James, it's a pleasure." His hand was planted before her, waiting for her acceptance.

Was he kidding? Did he not recognise her?

"Eva, dear, it's customary to shake a hand when presented. Especially the hand offered by his Royal Highness, Crown Prince Henrik of Stenaco." Prince Felix's words seemed far too casual to Eva. Like he knew.

Eva averted her gaze to the seam of Henrik's left shoulder before taking the hand before her. Her gut churned with unease. Executing a curtsy she hoped was satisfactory, she then dropped his hand like it was molten lava. *Crown Prince Henrik of Stenaco.* The words swam before her, her brain fuzzy as it tried to comprehend their meaning. The Henrik she'd known had never mentioned anything that even hinted at being royal, that he was in line to rule a small country. Hell, she thought he'd been a poor student like her, it was certainly how he'd acted.

Finding an inner strength, Eva's eyes flew back to his, searching, imploring him for any sign of recognition. How could he have forgotten her? Their time together, though short, had meant so much to her ... Deep down, she'd held on to the belief it had meant something to him too.

His lips became a flat line. Shuttered eyes met hers for a second then travelled over her shoulder. "Time to go, Felix. The limousine is waiting."

And that was that. The two men left with nothing more than a cursory nod from Felix, their bulky black shadows close behind.

Eva had dedicated hours of her life imagining the perfect scenario where she ran into Henrik. She often thought of all the reasons he'd never shown that night. She'd always shied away from the notion he'd been using her, that she'd misread his feelings. Had she just been a fun conquest to him? Something to joke about when he'd returned to his real life, how he'd duped a silly woman into falling for him without having to use his title? Of course, she'd made that pretty darn easy for him. More fool her.

On autopilot, Eva moved about the shop, flipping the closed sign and locking the front door. Placing one foot in front of the other, she trudged upstairs, seeking comfort from the worn leather of her sewing chair which sat nestled under the large-scale windows of the sitting room. The soft snores of her gramps were a relief, zipping through her chest. *At least I don't have to explain my closing early.* Eva stared at the gilt-edged fireplace that normally offered warmth and comfort, feeling numb. The light was too bright; the rug was so happy; the air was too fresh. Eva moulded her slim form into a ball, hoping she could roll away to the land of nothingness.

Five years hadn't diminished the invisible draw she felt whenever Henrik was nearby. His height still towered over hers, causing a feeling of fragility and femininity. His lips still looked like every taste of heaven. Eva closed her eyes and let the memories wash over her.

Eva had been roped into taking a week off to celebrate

her twenty-first birthday. Her friends had organised a miniscule apartment in Vernazza, part of the picturesque Cinque Terre region on Italy's coast. After a variety of harried train trips, with the last leg completed on a seemingly directionless bus, the girls had arrived tired and hungry. They'd been warned about the stairs required to reach their apartment so had decided to cure their hunger before attempting that feat.

Eva had been in a cloud of wonder since she'd stepped foot in the seaside village. The sun setting on the horizon, the vivid primary-coloured boats floating in the bay like little pieces of candy. Wafts of rich tomato and freshly caught fish enveloped her senses, enough to have her walking into a complete stranger. His strong arms had captured her fall, finding their way to her hips. She'd drowned in his sparkling eyes whilst he'd attempted to hold back his mirth.

Eva remembered how she'd felt disconnected, her limbs refusing to move from his grasp. Her lips had tingled from a need she'd never experienced before. Her already heightened senses had short-circuited from his touch. They'd only exchanged one word—his bemused warning for her to be 'careful' before he'd set her upright and walked off. She should have heeded his words.

Eva had eaten her meal, her eyes searching of their own accord for a certain pair of blue orbs. She'd barely remembered making her way up to the apartment before falling into a restless slumber.

Waking at dawn, unable to quiet the urge to go searching, she'd found herself once again down by the water. The night before, the area had been filled with wine and laughter; that morning held nothing but silence. The gentle lap of water offered a soothing contrast to the fast beat of her heart.

He sat on the rock wall as if waiting for her.

For five days, Eva had avoided her friends and fallen headlong into the world of Henrik. He'd professed to be a student, on a break from University. Away with friends just like her.

Every moment together had been filled with molten kisses and sighs, with only snippets of real life offered. Eva had never experienced that need before, the complete satisfaction from a physical connection.

She'd been the one to request they keep it light, no sharing of personal details, except even knowing next to nothing she'd fallen in love with him. When he'd asked her to meet him, the night before she was due to leave, she'd hoped it was to exchange details. A request to continue their affair, turn it into a real relationship.

Eva had waited. Three long hours as the sun vanished, and the moon exposed her foolishness.

Now she had proof that Henrik was never who she'd thought he was. And she was nothing to him at all—not even a memory.

Rain hammered against the limo's shaded windows, matching Prince Henrik's mood perfectly. Typical bloody London.

He shouldn't have come.

His brother had been acting weird lately, and this just proved he was up to something. If he hadn't agreed to collect Felix, he'd have never laid eyes on Eva again. She was a weakness he couldn't have in his life. A wish he could never fulfil.

"You're very quiet, brother dearest. Something on your mind?" Felix's words hung in the air, pointed with his knowing tone.

"No." Henrik's response was crisp. A silent request to cease any further questioning.

He adopted a bored expression and turned to face his younger brother. Envy washed through him. How nice it must be to have the title without the pressure. Whilst the brothers shared many similar physical traits, they couldn't be more polar opposites in personality. Felix's laid-back propensity for fun deeply contrasted Henrik's tightly held emotional reins. It was expected of him. From as early as he could remember, he knew he had to be just that bit better, more reserved, utterly calm, emotionless. The last time he'd let his true passions shine had been in Italy. Where he'd been able to truly be himself and immerse himself in the beauty and wonder that was Eva.

Then he'd received a sudden order to return home and watch his mother quietly die, her final words reminding him he had no place living a life of passion. Of love.

"So, are you staying at Lady Sophia's estate whilst we're in town?" Felix asked with an edge in his voice.

Henrik glanced over, taking in Felix's pinched features before his trademark lazy grin reappeared. What was that about? Henrik wondered if he'd imaged the look before dismissing the thought. "No, Sophia is visiting with friends in Monaco. I said I'd see her at the ball next month."

"Next month?" Felix's incredulous laugh followed his words. "That's some romance you got there, brother."

Henrik offered no response.

He knew the rumours circulated that he'd chosen Lady

Sophia to be his wife. He and Sophia had gotten a kick out of reading the delighted tales of royal romance and speculation on when the engagement would be announced. It would have to be soon; the pressure for him to marry was mounting, and Sophia was on the same page. Like him, she understood that duty came before freedom. They'd been friends a long time, and Henrik knew it would never be a great love story, but their betrothal would hopefully prove companionable.

His hands clenched at the thought. A burst of anger at his fate which he quelled with the ease of having done so a thousand times. His life was not his own, and he had long ago accepted that. It didn't mean he had to like it.

The car slowed to a stationary position. Not waiting for his bodyguard, he flung open his door, rain slashing across his face.

Unfolding his tall frame, he strode towards the palatial entrance of The London. Frank, the taller of his two ever-present bodyguards, attempted to shield him from the rainy skies with an umbrella. Pausing, Henrik let his gaze wander around him. Black skies, black-suited bodyguards, black umbrella. Black mood to seal it all. The thought had his lips twitching in a grimace before he resumed his march to the hotel lobby. Not stopping to acknowledge the manager who dashed towards him, or waiting for his brother, he took refuge in the elevator. Shoving his hands in his pockets, he let his lids shutter closed over tired eyes. Soaking in his five seconds of alone time, knowing his other set of bodyguards would be waiting by the penthouse doors, he gave in to temptation and let his mind drift back to Eva.

The years hadn't diminished her exquisite beauty. She was slimmer than he remembered, her natural grace clear in her movements. Her chocolate hair hung in straight locks, brushing against her shoulders. It was shorter than when he'd last seen her, when it had fallen in a glossy cascade down her back. Today she was dressed to work, crisp buttoned-up clothing hiding what he knew to be delectable curves. He could still bring to mind the sweet taste of her skin, her soft smiles and wondrous coffee-brown eyes. Those eyes had rattled him with confusion today when he'd pulled out his best acting to cloak their previous interactions.

He could have acknowledged knowing her, but really, what was the point? If they'd been alone, he knew he would have crumbled. His brother's presence had helped him stay strong. An ache settled in his chest at the deception, but it was for the best; she deserved better than him.

Ding. The elevator slid smoothly to a stop, drawing a line through his reminiscing. The silver doors slid apart to reveal his royal assistant impatiently tapping his foot, a tablet glued to his left hand as he furiously stabbed at the screen.

"Your Highness, your father has requested I review your schedule for the next few days. He has a few additional requests on your time whilst you're in London." Stefan gave a brief bow, then immediately launched into a quick step to match Henrik's. The man didn't draw breath before ticking off various new luncheon requests, breakfast meetings, and a formal dinner at the embassy. An overly full schedule would prove a welcome distraction from his thoughts on a certain brunette. He supposed he should ask Lady Sophia if she'd be available to fly in for the dinner but discarded the idea. Felix could come along. His brother's ability to turn over happy conversation with a stone would save Henrik from the boredom he knew would await them both. He stopped walking. Would he have been the more outgoing and personable son had he not been first born?

"Sir?"

Henrik heard his assistant but didn't answer, instead taking in his surroundings. He stood in the spacious sitting area of the penthouse, owned by the royal family especially for state visits like this. It was elegant, and to him, a home away from home. It had plush carpet, in parts covered by red and gold embroidered rugs—pieces that had been brought over from Stenaco. The furniture had been commissioned, hand-crafted, and approved by his mother. She'd loved decorating; it had been her passion. Her one outlet. She'd had the biggest smile when she saw the final version of this armchair ... it took her an age to choose where to place it. Moving it around to five different spots before setting it so it faced the windows. He ran a hand along the soft, slightly worn, fabric. He saw her in his mind, her expression carefree and filled with true happiness as she sat in this very spot. So different from her normally guarded face.

Why was he torturing himself with so many memories today?

Moving to the wall of windows, he gazed out at the cityscape that surrounded him. The London Eye sat square in his vision, its tiny bubbles moving in a slow circle, affording others a similar view to what he was seeing now. His country was not as big as England; its capital city, Geravia, was nowhere near as populated. But he loved his home, loved his country.

"Sir?" Stefan asked, concern entering his tone.

"Yes, Stefan." His words sounded dull even to his ears.

"Sorry, sir, but yes to which?"

He had no clue what Stefan was talking about. He turned towards his assistant, his right eyebrow quirked in question. Stefan fidgeted with the switch at the side of the tablet. A worried frown showed on his face as he opened his mouth a few times.

"Stefan, I have no idea what you are asking. Please accept my apologies. I was not listening." Henrik sank into the lush claret coloured leather couch. The smooth coldness enveloped his form, leaving him wishing the marble fireplace was lit.

Stefan's frown deepened.

"Is everything all right, Your Highness? Shall I have a doctor summoned?"

"No, Stefan. I'm not sick." *Not a sickness that a doctor could cure, anyway.* "Please start again. I promise this time you have my full attention."

Stefan's look was dubious.

"Full attention, Stefan. You have my word."

Hooking his left ankle across his right knee, Henrik focused his mind. He'd had his five minutes of distraction.

Time to go back to being the crown prince.

2

———————

va woke to a loud banging. Shaking the fuzziness from her mind, she wondered at how easily she'd drifted off. Too many late nights catching up coupled with this afternoon's emotional blow. Cursing her stupidity, she unfolded the kinks in her back as she headed for the front door of the shop, hoping to stop the banging before it also woke her gramps.

Flicking the lock, she was faced with a burly man dressed in a smart black suit. "May I help you?"

"Miss James?"

She gave a single nod in response.

"Prince Felix of Stenaco has requested I deliver these documents to you personally, miss." An oversized hand stretched a wax sealed maroon envelope in her direction. She accepted it with a slight nod, focusing on the royal insignia embossed on the card front. Flicking the flap open, she saw a handwritten note shoved in the front. Her heart skipped, indecision flooding her. Was it from Henrik? Her hand wavered before snatching out the piece of paper. A brief glance doused her suspicion. A flamboyant signature lay at the bottom starting with an F. No H in sight. Her stomach dipped as unwanted disappointment set in. *Stupid heart.* She looked up to thank the messenger, but he was already driving off.

Well. Felix was true to his word at least. Not that it mattered. He could issue a million job offers to her, but there was no way she'd be accepting any position that put her near Henrik. After seeing him look through her like she was absolutely nothing she knew she needed to move on. She didn't understand how he could have forgotten their time together? Had she meant that little to him?

"Eva? Who was at the door?"

The croaky words intercepted her pensive mood. Moving to the stairs, she took her gramps' gnarled hand and helped him back in the direction he'd come from.

"You needn't have gotten up, Gramps. It was just a courier." Eva tried to keep the chiding tone prominent in her voice, hiding her worry.

Directing him over to the matching leather chair that sat next to hers, she tucked him in under the woollen throw. Swamped by bold, rich colour, he looked small and fragile. His white wispy hair thinned atop his head, offering the perfect spot for her to place a gentle kiss. Tossing the papers on her own chair, she moved to light the fire.

"Are you done fussing now?" Gramps' tone had turned sulky.

Eva regarded his sullen frown for a moment before grinning. "You know I'm never done fussing." She checked the silver antique watch that sat upon her slim wrist. The day had gotten away from her. She'd organise dinner before making a start on the long evening of stitching required to finish the prince's order. She would have the suit couriered over in the morning, include a regretful note regarding the job, and that would be that. *Goodbye, Henrik.* She tried to ignore the hit her heart took at the thought.

"Eva, dear, you look lost."

She swallowed before answering. "No Gramps, not at all. Just mentally planning my evening. I have an order that needs finishing."

"Child, you're taking on too much. You do nothing but work and look after me."

"That's not true."

"When was the last time you went out?" Her silence spoke volumes. "You're only young once, Eva. You need to go live."

"I will, once you're back on your feet." She knew the words were a lie. Going out just didn't interest Eva; she had her work, and any spare time she used to sketch new designs. Designing had always been her passion, but it was a fanciful dream, one she'd never follow. Her life was happy enough.

"You and I both know that's nonsense. I may be old but I'm not stupid. You're overworking yourself to keep the business alive."

Eva opened her mouth to reply but paused when he lifted his hand in front of her.

"Don't deny it, please. This conversation is long overdue. The business has been losing clients for years. We aren't big enough to remain competitive like some of the other old guys on the block, and they are noticing a decline too. Your work is some of the finest I've ever seen, but this industry is a name game—it always has been. And I'm afraid our name just isn't cutting it anymore."

Panic gripped Eva. How many hits did she have to take today? She slowly massaged each of her fingers, one by one, loosening the kinks that formed at the end of every day.

Hundreds of stitches were required in every jacket order, every waistband, every hem, every button-hole. And every one she did by hand. That was her job. It was her gramps' business; she couldn't let it just slip away.

"Are those papers from the bank?" Gramps' words held strength, like he'd been working up to this question, the one he'd really wanted to ask.

Eva looked at the offending papers. No, those weren't from the bank, but the pile of unpaid bills hidden in her work drawer downstairs told her she'd be getting bank papers soon too. Another pile of paper to shatter her.

A chill skittered down her spine that the fire could do nothing to dissipate. "No, they aren't. I need to go get dinner started. I'll be right back."

Needing some distance from the conversation, Eva headed to the small kitchenette just off the lounge room. You'd never swing a cat in there, but it was functional.

The fridge showed slim pickings, but she located frozen soup, mentally adding meal planning to her list. When was the last time she'd cleaned the kitchen? Perhaps that should go on the list too. Even her thoughts sounded melancholy. Was Gramps right? Was she really living, or just going through the motions?

A muffled cough sounded from the kitchen doorway.

"A royal appointment?" Her gramps' eyes shone with pride.

Dropping her head back against the cupboard, Eva rolled her eyes to the ceiling. She should have known his curiosity would get the better of him.

"I've said no." Or she would do, first thing in the morning.

"Why on earth would you turn this down? Eva, dear, this is a chance of a lifetime." Gramps shuffled forward, taking her hand in his, the rough pads of his fingertips, studded with needle pricks rubbed against hand. She knew her own headed that way. "What are you so afraid of?"

'*Having my heart broken further*' was the answer that whispered in her mind. Drawing her eyebrows together she shrugged. "I'm not afraid. The timing is just... not right. You're not well and the business won't run itself."

Gramps excitement faded into a frown. His mouth drew a flat line. "You've turned this down to stay with the family business. To look after me?"

"It's what I want."

"Is it? I can keep the business ticking over. We aren't that inundated with orders. I can quote longer turn-around times. I'm not dismissing the work you do, but this is an opportunity you *must* consider."

Leaning forward, Eva drew him in for a hug, seeking comfort as much as offering a silent apology. Yes, it was what she wanted. What she needed. She couldn't risk taking a job that put her within breathing distance of Henrik, not after today. Besides which, even if Henrik wasn't part of the equation, her gramps wasn't well. She couldn't possibly consider abandoning him right now, regardless of his claims that he'd cope without her.

"Before you continue that thought any further, I can have a nurse come take care of me, get some form of in-home care. You don't need to worry about leaving me alone to fend for myself. My old body will heal, hell it's only a bit of pneumonia. I promise I'll be fine without you."

Eva pursed her lips, dubious at his claims and a little put out that he'd so easily read her mind.

"Go take a seat, dinner's nearly ready."

He narrowed his eyes before he shuffled back out of the kitchen, muttering about youth and stupidity. Her lips twitched in amusement before settling into a slight frown. She was doing the right thing.

After dinner, Eva left her gramps to his murder mystery show. Collecting the contract, she hid downstairs, deciding to sew to the peaceful strains of Beethoven's many symphonies. Normally she'd keep Gramps company but tonight she wanted solitude. He'd attempted to discuss the contract twice during dinner and Eva had no strength left to argue.

Her documents drawer protested loudly as she slid it out, the red stamped 'overdue' notice capturing her gaze. She'd taken the prince's short-notice appointment just after that bill had arrived. She didn't have answers for the four similar bills that hid beneath it.

Eva fingered the corners of each bill before laying them out. The papers covered the worst of the ancient table marks but revealed new wounds; the business was in serious trouble. The royal embellished maroon card that sat atop the prince's half sewn jacket mocked her predicament.

Why did life have to be so cruel? Before her lay the answer to her problems but how could she accept the position, knowing Henrik would be at the palace? How on earth would she maintain any professionalism? She'd been left wondering for five years why he walked out on their love whilst he'd clearly not given her one thought. Snatching up the folder she laid it across the bills, knowing she'd never settle into her work until she knew the offer details.

It didn't take long for her eyes to pick out the important details. Short-term contract based at the palace in Geravia, capital city of Stenaco; all food, accommodation, transportation inclusive; carte blanch for fabric choice. A generous salary on top of the extras she'd already mentally noted.

She let out a low whistle. It was an extravagant offer

considering the prince had only met her twice. Would the role include tailoring for other members of the family or just Prince Felix? Not that it mattered, seeing as she wasn't taking the job.

Slamming the folder shut, Eva drummed her fingers on the front cover, her gaze drawn to the royal insignia. The scripted *S* was surrounded by floral indents. One word, Stenaco, cut through the middle with swirls at either end. It was beautiful. Her index finger traced each line, each swirl.

"I have to know." Her words broke the silence. Fishing out her laptop, she tapped in a few select words and was bombarded with images of Henrik. A very different-looking Henrik to the one who featured in her memories. The man who looked back at her was the Henrik she'd met today, whose emotionless face and blank eyes looked every bit the royal prince she now knew him to be.

A headline caught Eva's eye, including close-up images of a beautiful blonde heiress encircled within Henrik's arms. *'Lady Sophia and Prince Henrik danced the night away at her cousin's wedding ... Could that be practice for their own nuptials?'*

Eva's fragile heart sank. He was engaged. To an ivory-skinned, serene, perfect-looking woman who had a title and knew how to mingle in the company of royals. It was no wonder he didn't remember her. She was way outside this Lady Sophia's league; hell, she wasn't even close to that playing field. She sewed for a living. Most of her wardrobe she'd made herself. She'd bet good money Lady Sophia's wardrobe was filled with Prada, Chanel and Dior.

Looking again at the overdue bills, then the contract, Eva made the choice she'd been dreading. She'd take the role. She was letting a fantasy stand in the way of a real-life chance. She could shove her emotions aside—she'd been doing it for five years. Surely now it would be easier. Henrik wasn't coming to find her. He was royalty and appeared to be in love with someone else.

As her gramps' had pointed out, he could still do some of the sewing. The job was only for a month, so it wasn't even that long. Collecting her diary she flicked through the upcoming weeks, her heart hardening as page after page was blank. There were a few appointments, but she could start a lot of that work before she left, leaving as little sewing as possible for her gramps. Mainly regulars whose measurements and patterns were already on file. Felix's appointment and a walk-in last week were the only new clients they'd had this month. Out of the ordinary appointments which had kept her busy but there was no guarantee that would happen again next week. The company finances were *not* a pretty picture.

If she could take this royal appointment in Stenaco, she'd be able to use the money to buy the business some time, to find ways to drum up more clientele. She could do some advertising, certainly something they hadn't been able to afford. She could pay her friend, Annette, who was a nurse, to check in on her gramps until his pneumonia was cleared. The doctor had cleared him to be at home and to do some work. It had been her insisting he spend all his time resting.

Did she really have a choice?

She'd move on, grasp this opportunity and use the money to save her gramps' business.

It wouldn't hold the wolves at bay eternally, but it'd buy her the time she needed. Gramps had given her everything —this was her chance to return the favour.

Eva looked up at number twenty-two Savile Row—at the royal blue door—one last time before she folded herself into the taxi. Asking to be taken to the airport she texted her friend, letting her know she was on her way and triple checking the details for her gramps care. By seven p.m. this evening she'd be in Geravia, the capital city of Stenaco. She'd be a guest of the palace, living in Henrik's home for the next month. Her heart had not settled since she'd couriered over Felix's suit and her acceptance of his offer. Would it ever settle again?

3

"Thanks for cutting your trip short to come here, Sophia. I appreciate it."

Sophia let out a short laugh. "You make it sound like some big favour. You know I'm happy to come here to the palace anytime. Anything to get away from Mummy." She mock shuddered.

"She's still driving you insane then?"

"My mother will drive me insane from the grave, I'm sure of it." Sophia's mouth tightened into a grim line.

Henrik's eyebrows lifted in surprise. "Bit morbid. Has something else happened between you two?"

"Nothing out of the ordinary but let's not discuss my mother, please. I'd far rather hear why you suddenly needed me to come to Stenaco?"

Henrik paused, letting the midday sun soak the skin on his face. He'd left his suit jacket inside, keen to take a walk with Sophia and cement a few details of their upcoming engagement announcement. He'd love to roll up the sleeves of his shirt, loosen his tie just a little and properly breathe

the fresh air but he didn't dare risk it. It wouldn't do for him to be seen in such a casual state.

Sophia had paused also, looking out at the gardens that lay stretched before them. They'd chosen to walk the path that ran closest to the palace, but as it sat uphill, they'd be visible to any overeager photographers outside the wrought-iron palace walls. Henrik turned to look at Sophia. She was every bit the picture of sophistication and grace an English lady should be. Every bit the perfect candidate for his wife, to eventually become queen of Stenaco. They'd been friends since the moment they could talk. She was one of the few people he trusted.

When she'd come to him asking for help to find someone to marry, he'd thought it the perfect solution for them both. A marriage of friendship and respect. He loved her, as a friend, but it wasn't the great romance the media often tried to turn it into. Or any romance at all. Henrik made sure no stories released in Stenaco put that spin on it. They would marry, Stenaco would have its future, and Henrik would have a stronger reason to forget Eva.

He laughed grimly at the thought. Forgetting her hadn't been easy for the past five years, how would marrying another woman make it any easier? But it must. Seeing her in London, whilst painful, had renewed his resolve to make the best choice. Eva deserved happiness, a life she could lead however she wanted. Being with him wouldn't lead to happiness.

"Earth to Henrik?" Sophia poked him in the arm, a concerned look on her face. "Where did I lose you to? Perhaps the reason for my summoning?"

Henrik shook off his mood. "Summoning? I did no such thing. We both know no one could ever make you do something you didn't want to. Well, except maybe your mother."

She narrowed her eyes at him. "Fine, I'll call a truce on asking questions on the strange change in plans. You're acting out of character, but I'll bide my time and get the full story out of you later." Her words were glib, her voice confident.

Henrik didn't like her chances. He'd told no one about Eva—well, not the full story anyway, even though he'd never ceased thinking about her. Her name constantly popped into his mind, her image swimming on the backs of his eyelids from the moment he woke and as he went to sleep each night. Each day he thought he'd do better, that he'd learn to forget her, and each day he failed. It was an impossible situation. Why couldn't he force his heart to understand that?

Henrik pulled his phone from his pocket, shooting a quick text to Stefan to find time in his diary for a chat with Felix. Off-loading some steam at his brother's lack of concern for their royal duties should help.

"Are you okay if we head towards the rose garden maze? I know it brings back memories ..." Henrik's breath whooshed out like he'd been kicked in the stomach by a stallion, taken off guard by Sophia's request. It shouldn't still matter, but thinking of the garden, so close to thoughts of Eva, sent his mind into a further downward spiral.

"Sure." The word was clipped, hiding any emotion in his response. He fingered the smooth surface of the phone before shoving it, along with his hands, into the pockets of his tailored trousers. His shoulders hunched slightly, and he had to physically force himself to relax. He knew if his father saw him, there'd be a lecture. No prince should walk around slouched with his hands in his pockets. But screw it.

"Izzie sent a message about drinks tonight. A new club she's been dying to check out. Are you keen?"

Not really, was his initial thought. But that wasn't fair to Sophia so instead he nodded in agreement, knowing he should also pay more attention to his younger sister Isabella when she was out and about.

The path wound around a corner, revealing crisp white stone steps back up into the palace, steps he desperately wished to take. But he moved towards the maze, his eyes tracking the ground. He didn't need to look up to see the intricate lilac ironwork formed into an arch that indicated the entrance. The smell of roses hit him like a punch to the face, their perfume permeating the air a good five metres away.

The effect of the roses always caught him off guard, but it paled to nothing compared to the impact of seeing Eva standing at the entrance to the maze. Shock froze him to the spot, his head swimming.

What was she doing here?

His heart beat faster, almost as if it would jump out and go find its one and only true owner. Had he been thinking of her so much that he'd conjured her from nowhere?

It took him a moment to realise Felix was standing beside her, greeting Sophia, who was looking back at him curiously. His brain had disconnected. He was unable to take a step forward or backwards, glued to the spot. Why on earth was Eva standing in front of his mother's rose garden? What was she doing in Stenaco?

Desire warred with panic at the thought of being close to her again. Of having her in his beloved country. He'd dreamt of such a picture, only in his mind, in the depths of the night, memories of their time together blocked out his very real concerns, his reasons for walking away from her. In the light of day there was no way he could hide from his resolve.

"Oh, what a gorgeous dress!"

Sophia's words jarred into his mind, breaking the spell. He stripped all emotion from his face, barricading himself behind his usual crown mask. His movements were economical, stopping beside Sophia.

"Brother, you remember Eva, don't you?" The words stung—not that he allowed it to show. Felix's use of her first name didn't bode well.

"Miss James, welcome to Stenaco." He couldn't be sure, but she appeared to flinch at his greeting. Her eyes wouldn't meet his, though Henrik was quietly thankful for that. Drowning in her eyes was something he remembered all too easily. "May I present Lady Sophia?"

Eva's mouth pulled into a slight smile as she nodded.

Felix raised an eyebrow at Henrik, finding his own amusement in the situation. "So formal, as always. Guess that's why they call you Prince Perfect."

Henrik wanted to grimace at the term but resisted. Felix was playing a game of some sort, Henrik would bet money on it. "At least someone is acting like a prince and taking their job seriously. I spent half of yesterday entertaining the dignitaries from Monaco, a job I believe Father requested you do."

Silence stretched for a moment at the gauntlet Henrik had thrown before Felix erupted into laughter. The noise grated on Henrik's nerves. Were his words wise? Probably not. He'd never before voiced disapproval at Felix's lack of consideration for his princely duties. He'd just picked up the slack and moved on. But he was getting tired of always carrying the heavy duties whilst Felix cavorted about the place with different women. He was man enough to admit this particular interest in Eva was the final straw.

Sophia's head bobbed from one man to the other,

concern written across her features. "Eva, please excuse these boys, I'm not sure what's gotten into them today." She flashed a warning look at both Henrik and Felix before continuing. "You must tell me more about your dress."

Henrik had avoided looking directly at Eva after his initial glimpse and shock, but with Sophia's words, his gaze was drawn to the dress in question. It was ivory, accenting the silky skin it covered. It skimmed her form ending in some sort of frill. The neckline sat up slightly, curving over her shoulders and towards her back. She used to love kisses at the base of her neck. The dress was simple but something about the fit and how it moulded to Eva's frame was striking. Henrik's fingers itched to reach out, stroke a hand along the dress, feeling the woman beneath it. He scrunched his hands into fists, hooking them behind his back.

Henrik lifted his eyes to her face. Wisps of her hair had escaped the up-do and fluttered in the slight breeze. Her eyes darted from his, a slight rosy tinge appearing in her cheeks. She opened her mouth to speak when Felix jumped in first.

"Eva designed it herself. She's here as my tailor. Extremely talented—I couldn't help but coerce her into working here for a short stint. Of course, I hope it'll be longer, but she's proving difficult to tie down." Felix's gaze swung briefly to Henrik.

"A tailor? That explains the exquisite fit." Sophia's smile was warm and genuine. "I'd love to see any other designs you have. I'm on the board at the British Fashion Council— we're always looking to support new talent. Where are you based?"

Henrik was drinking in Eva's features, surprised she was still silent but not surprised at the shock shining on her face at Sophia's words. He knew they'd mean a lot to Eva. Well, the Eva he'd known five years ago anyway. Her talent and obvious pleasure in designing was one of the few personal subjects they'd discussed. Henrik had often caught himself going to google her name, to see if she'd pursued her dreams past working as a tailor. He'd always stopped himself, believing he'd be better off knowing nothing.

He needed to go. Standing this close to Eva was doing his head in. "Miss James is very talented. If you'll excuse me, Stefan is hyperventilating at the window." Henrik marched away without waiting for a reply, cursing himself for letting those words out.

The sound of jogging and his name being called, halted his stride. As much as he wanted to forge ahead and ignore his brother, his ingrained manners had finally kicked in.

"That was very fine praise for someone you've barely met ... twice." Felix's eyes were searching, squinting, like he was asking a different question to the one he voiced.

Henrik refused to be baited. "I was being courteous. Did you check with anyone before hiring a new tailor? Lorenzo has been working for this family since before we were born. I hope you're not ruffling feathers with this stunt." Bite crept into his words.

"Yes *father*, I checked. Lorenzo has heard of James Tailoring; he's on board with my decision to bring Eva to stay here for the next month. Perhaps she could even make something for you—help decrease that stuffiness you hide behind." Sarcasm dripped from Felix's words.

"Staying here, as in, at the palace, you mean?"

"Yes. What of it?"

Panic gripped Henrik. He took a deep breath before gritting his teeth and uttering his fears. "Felix, you might want to stop and think about how that will look to the media— you bringing an attractive young woman from London to stay at the palace. Make sure you send a press release. I'm sure Miss James doesn't want any unwarranted media coverage linking her as one of your latest conquests!" His words were terse, trying to cover his fear with anger.

"Now, now, brother, I don't meddle with your love life. Why should you butt into mine?"

Henrik used all his experience to tamp down the rage that flashed through him at his brother's insinuation. He needed to go, compose himself before he did something he'd later regret. Like punch his brother in the face.

4
___

*E*va watched the exchange between the brothers, desperate to know what they were discussing. Seeing Henrik so soon after arriving in his country had rendered her speechless. Her heart was not at all prepared for their interaction, nor for seeing Lady Sophia, who was so different to what Eva had imagined. Granted they'd only spoken for a few minutes, but Sophia radiated such an open and friendly nature, Eva could only conclude she was a long way from some of the other snobbish, titled ladies she'd met before.

Henrik balled his hands into fists. Was he going to punch his brother? His face was a mask but even from this distance she could see anger radiating from those blue eyes. But why? Was she the cause? She could barely make heads or tails of this situation. He'd appeared tense when he'd first seen her, then angry at Felix, but then he'd been complimentary about her work. Did Henrik remember her after all and his anger at Felix was because he'd bought her here?

Hurt at the direction her thoughts were taking, Eva closed her eyes briefly before focusing on her shoes. She couldn't bear to watch him walk away from her again. The thought sat in her mind for a moment before she flicked it away. She was moving on, remember? Just because her heart wasn't on the same page yet, didn't matter. She'd get it there. She was standing with the woman Henrik was in love with. If that wasn't a reminder of the prince's true loyalties, nothing was.

"It's a beautiful maze. Did you make it to the wisteria pergola at the centre?"

Eva looked up to find Sophia's gaze locked firmly on hers, scrutinising.

Eva stammered a reply, glad of the mundane subject. "Um, no. I haven't been in yet actually." Was that the best she could do? "I've found the rest of the gardens wonderful so far. They are very inspiring." Okay, not much better. She'd never been good at small talk.

"Yes, it was their mother's garden. She used to love purple, hence the wisteria at its centre." Sadness crossed Sophia's face before she cleared it. "Maybe you'll find some inspiration for your designs? I really would love to talk to you more about your work. I could go ring for coffee, or tea if you prefer it?"

"Oh, thanks, but actually, I had best wait for Felix. I need to discuss my lodgings here. There was a mix-up with the room they've put me in." Eva's gaze tracked back to the palace, searching ...

"What's wrong with the room you've been given?" Felix jogged back into their conversation, apparently hearing her last comment.

Eva felt silly being so easily distracted by Henrik when she should be focused on the job she was being paid to do.

"I might leave you to it." Sophia said, smiling at Eva. "Oh actually, Izzie has organised drinks tonight, Felix. You should bring Eva. It would be nice for her to do something other than work whilst she's visiting."

Eva watched Sophia walk away, elegance radiating like a halo around her. She managed to hold in a sigh, knowing she'd never achieve that type of composure.

She turned back to Felix, determination replacing her envy, but she was brought up short at the thoughtful look on Felix's face as his gaze followed Sophia's back. Odd, seeing as he'd barely looked Sophia's way when she and Henrik had come across them. It was almost like he'd avoided looking at her. Eva shelved the information for later. Right now, she needed some answers.

"Your Highness, are you sure I've been put in the correct room?"

"I thought we agreed on Felix? The formality gets boring." His response sounded as if he were a little distracted, which annoyed Eva. She was starting to feel like she was just here for some game she didn't have the rules for.

"Okay, Felix. Can you please spare me five minutes to discuss some questions I have?" The words were said through gritted teeth.

He turned his head to Eva, offering a genuine smile. "Of course. All the time in the world for you, Eva darling. But first let me show you the maze. The fresh air is wonderful for the soul."

Eva didn't particularly care for a walk. She wanted to get on with her work. Since landing in this country last night she'd done nothing but sit in the suite she'd been given, feeling lost and overwhelmed by the opulence. She needed direction, to get back to a level footing. Work was something she knew how to do, something she could lose her mind in. Something to distract her thoughts from Henrik. Felix had checked in this morning after breakfast but had been vague about the job and had deflected her attempts to discuss specifics.

"Sure, a walk would be nice. But can we talk about the room, please? It seems overly large for work quarters."

Overly large was an understatement. The bedroom was bigger than her gramps' entire apartment. A balcony with picturesque mountain views ran its length. An adjoining room was fitted with everything she'd need to work as a tailor. The luxury of the walk-in robe and en suite had made her want to cry. She'd been waiting for someone to come tell her there'd been a mistake.

Felix shrugged in response, already leading the way towards the maze entrance. Eva struggled to keep up in her heels. They were only moderate height, part of her professional look, but it seemed Felix was on a mission.

"Is the room okay? Does it have all the tools you need?" He threw an enquiring glance her way.

"Yes, it's more than okay. I just worried there was a mistake."

"Why?"

"Because it's huge."

Felix seemed preoccupied with his thoughts. His brows were drawn, hands shoved into black dress pants. His normal, carefree air seemed to have evaporated.

"It's a guest room, Eva; that's just how they come. I took the liberty of arranging some additional clothing to be placed in the walk-in robe. I hope you don't mind. I guessed your size."

Eva missed a step, fumbling on the pebbled pathway. That explained why those clothes were in there. She'd drooled over the designer pieces but hadn't had the nerve to touch anything for fear she had stumbled into someone else's closet. Felix's words were giving her serious pause. As was his unnatural fast pace and the way he kept rubbing at the back of his neck.

"Why did you buy me clothes?"

"I thought you might like them." The words were casual and thrown over his shoulder as he continued to march with purpose to some unknown destination.

"Your Highness, please stop. What's going on?" Eva tried to keep the frustration from her voice. She lifted her chin, her bottom lip finding its way beneath her teeth.

Eva watched as Felix spun towards her, his eyes partially meeting hers before skirting away. He paced around the short space, each step bringing his eyebrows closer together before coming to stand before her. The two stood in silence, facing each other, before Felix quirked a smile.

"I thought we agreed you'd call me Felix."

"We did. We also agreed I was here as your tailor, yet I'm in a guest suite larger than my home and you've bought me clothing. Why?"

Sighing, Felix rubbed a hand over the stubble on his jaw.

"Okay, it seems it's time for my confession. I know the contract says I've hired you as my tailor, but I hope to talk you into acting as my girlfriend instead."

Eva's shock must have been written on her face, because Felix held his hand up before he continued. "For appearances only. I ... need a cover from a particularly avaricious ex."

"So, you want to pay me to be your girlfriend?" Eva wasn't sure she liked the sound of that. Why her? What would Henrik think?

"Yes."

"That's crazy. I'm a tailor, a nobody. Who'd believe *us*?"

"Well, it's the perfect reason for us meeting. We can say I fell for you on the spot. And, to be honest, it works in our favour that no one knows you."

No one except Henrik.

Eva couldn't stop the voice that shouted in her head. Would this charade make him jealous? Would he care? Why, oh why, couldn't she stop thinking about him? He was off-limits to her.

"No." The word escaped her lips before she could stop it, her heart not waiting for any decision that came from her head.

"Please, Eva. I'll double the money. Triple it if I have too."

The offer lay between them, a sum of money large enough to have Eva gulping for breath. It also left a bad taste in her mouth. Something wasn't adding up about Felix's suggestion. If he wanted her to act as his girlfriend, why hadn't he just asked her upfront? Why the charade of a job contract? Why throw that kind of money at her when she knew he'd have a little black book full of names just waiting for his call?

"You could use the opportunity to showcase your designs. I saw you scribbling away on the plane, and admit that I snuck a glance when you were in the bathroom. You're a very talented tailor, but your passion for designing transformed your face—you glowed with happiness. Your designs are pure talent. I can help you."

His new suggestion caused Eva to freeze. Felix was astute. She dreamed of seeing her designs come to life, being worn by the rich and famous. Heck, being worn by anyone but her. If she could, she'd open her own label, but it just wasn't on the cards.

"I seem to have robbed you of words for the moment. I'll leave you to have a wander and think it over."

Eva didn't know what to think. She didn't want to become a pawn in some game. Taking the position of Felix's girlfriend, albeit briefly, would surely throw her into Henrik's path constantly. She wasn't sure she had the strength to handle that, but on the other hand, could she really walk away from the much-needed money?

She took in a deep breath. An intoxicating perfume swamped the air, bringing her focus back to her surroundings. A sea of purple blooms draped from the pristine marble columns, making Eva assume they'd reached the pinnacle of the maze.

The different hues and textures had Eva itching for her notebook. Her mind immediately shaped a dreamy gown— yards of silk satin, drifting into a train coated with embroidered flowers, or perhaps on the underside so the wearer looked to be walking in a field of blooms.

Her suits were an art form, she'd been told as much many times, but to her they were a dull form of art. They were functional, not at all the frivolous beauty she wanted to create. Could she pull this charade off? Did she want to put herself that close to Henrik? What if he did remember her? Would it help her move on?

"Wait." The word was whispered from her dry mouth. She swallowed, trying to shift the cotton ball that had lodged in the back of her throat. Their agreement would need to be clear—girlfriend on paper only. Still, she knew there was a good chance she'd regret her next words. "Okay, I'll do it."

Henrik sat in the limousine, shifting to find a more comfortable position. Sophia had kindly informed him she'd extended the invitation for drinks to Eva, unknowingly putting him into an afternoon of hell. He'd considered begging off, but then changed his mind. Eva was in no way his, but he needed to warn her off Felix. She was too trusting and too innocent to be wrapped up in one of his brother's games.

Felix dated women like most people changed their socks —frequently and without thought. It was a harsh assessment, but in the past few years Felix had ramped up his dating escapades and it was starting to reflect badly in the press.

He looked at Sophia sitting beside him, her normal serene self. It wouldn't have been a good look for him if Sophia had arrived in the country this morning and then he hadn't come with her this evening. The press could be vicious, he knew the consequences of how bad they could be. He needed to make sure that nothing he did was out of the ordinary. His behaviour must be exemplary, and true to form. He tried to focus on that, not how he wanted to talk to Eva alone.

The door opened. A delicate ankle ending in a blindingly pink heel appeared, followed by the rest of Eva's long legs and desirable body. Henrik had to forcibly stop himself reaching out to touch her, to help her inside the vehicle. She wore slim black pants and a high-neck silky top, her hair slightly tousled and framing a face with minimal makeup. Nothing overtly sexy. In fact, minus the shoes, she could be dressed for work. She was smiling when she dropped into the seat, looking back towards his sister, Izzie, who hopped in next, followed last by Felix.

Henrik waited for Eva to look up. He'd spent the afternoon in flux, for the first time in his life unsure how to approach a situation. He was astute enough to realise Eva very much remembered him, and was confused by his behaviour so far.

A part of him was desperate to apologise. For pretending to not know her in London, and for never turning up all those years ago. She deserved an explanation, but could he dredge up all the awful memories of his mother's last words and explain?

It wouldn't change his position. Her being in Stenaco and staying at the palace would be torture. Knowing she was within arm's reach but so very far off limits. He'd settled on warning her off Felix, she could do her job and he'd stay as far away as possible. He was determined to maintain a professional demeanour.

Chocolate eyes locked with his, surprise evaporating the carefree happiness he'd seen there moments ago. He nodded, not trusting any words out of his mouth. Her eyes held a tinge of sadness before determination lit them with a renewed sparkle. A tight smile formed at her lips, then she bowed her head, fidgeting with the silver bracelet at her wrist. It was the only piece of jewellery she wore, a piece he recognised.

The bracelet *he'd* bought for her in Corniglia, years ago, the day after they'd met. He'd wanted her to have it, so she'd have something to remind her of him and their time together. Already he'd felt their connection was special, like two souls who were destined to love and had found one another. He couldn't believe she'd kept it.

"Henrik, we're going to a nightclub not a state dinner. Don't you own casual clothes?" His sister's cheeky tone broke the torrent of memories that had flashed in his mind from that one piece of jewellery.

"Yes, I do. They didn't seem appropriate." He sounded stuffy and boring, but that was who he was. The country had certain expectations for their crown prince that simply didn't apply to his siblings.

His pint-sized sister was the spitting image of their mother, yet her personality was more like a soda stream of bubbles. Their mother had held a quiet humour, an inner peace and strength he'd admired and drawn from—support he missed every day.

"Let's open some bubbles, kick off this party properly." Felix followed his words by fishing out a bottle of Cristal from the side fridge of the limousine, expertly opening it and then handing around glasses. Felix paused a little when he reached Henrik, smirking as he held out the glass. Henrik didn't hesitate, taking the glass offered, ignoring the raised brow directed his way. Having Eva seated so close, combined with his sister's comment and brother's relentless teasing, made him question whether everyone perceived him to be uptight. Did Eva think he was a total stick in the mud too?

Izzie hooked her spare arm through Eva's, pulling her against her side like they'd known each other for years. Eva's eyes widened slightly, but only Henrik seemed to notice. She shifted her heels around, like she was nervous. Tension clutched at Henrik. Was she becoming overwhelmed? His body ached to reach out, take her hand, and tell her ... what? That it would be okay? He took a sip of the bubbles, trying to relax his shoulders.

Henrik ordered his gaze from Eva, instead taking in the others. Felix draining his glass of champagne, Sophia smiling at something Izzie was telling her, Izzie animated in talk of a new dress. His eyes followed each of them before landing back on Eva, willing her to look up. But she resolutely kept her gaze on her own glass, refusing to look his way.

Henrik had only been given vague details about the club they were headed to and was shocked when the limo pulled up to a sea of reporters. Usually they were left relatively alone when going anywhere in Geravia, but this group looked almost like they were waiting for something. Or someone. Felix was out the door in a flash, gallantly leaning in to help the ladies alight.

With the others out of the car, Henrik was alone with Eva for the first time in five years. She slowed, turning towards him like she was going to say something, then appeared to change her mind.

"Eva, wait. You still have it."

Her eyes flicked straight to her wrist. "Yes. It was too beautiful to part with." Her eyes raised to his, so many questions swimming in their depths.

He wanted to still time. The urge to lean over and pull the door closed, to keep Eva all to himself, was so strong he wondered that his limbs didn't move by themselves. He wanted to erase time, go back to Italy and the bubble of happiness they'd found there.

Felix's head popped back into the doorway. "Something the matter?"

It snapped the connection. Eva hurried out of the car with Felix's helping hand.

Henrik was left to move through a cloud of her perfume, his senses drinking in the light floral scent. She hadn't changed it; the overtones of gardenia and lemon were still as refreshing as his memories of Italy.

He dragged himself from the vehicle as flashes sparkled in the cool night. It took him a moment to realise they weren't pointed at him, but at the couple before him, locked in a theatrical embrace that wiped all thoughts and feelings from his body. The delicious scent of Eva's perfume was replaced by the scent of media hunger, thirsting for a story. Words were being shouted. He struggled to puzzle them together, his brain going into lockdown as he interpreted the picture before him. Felix kissing a dark-haired woman, dipping her in a Hollywood move, his arm clutching the slim black leg that ended in a lollipop pink heel.

Felix kissing Eva.

Bile rose in this throat, his limbs heavier than lead.

"Henrik, you might want to wipe that look from your face before one of the photographers captures you." Sophia whispered urgently at his ear. His common sense slammed back into place along with his neutral mask. Whatever this hell was, he needed to get away, find some space to get his wits back together. Find something heavier to drink than a damn glass of champagne.

Then he needed to speak to Eva.

5
———

*E*va resisted the urge to swipe her hand over her lips. The kiss had been a total surprise, Felix's mouth had been on hers before she'd realised what was happening. Now she stood with his arm about her waist, within a media snowstorm. The flashes and calls for details on who she was made her nervous; her pounding heart and glazed eyes probably appeared lovestruck to the camera lens. But to Eva they were driven from a total feeling of being out of her depth. How did people live like this?

Her eyes searched of their own accord for Henrik, whose back she could glimpse through the crowd that had formed around Prince Felix and herself. He was escorting Lady Sophia inside the club, as he should be, but it didn't stop the pang to her heart at seeing his arm about another woman's waist.

Felix gave a little jab to her hip, and she realised she was meant to be answering questions. The frigid air wasn't doing anything to cool the heat that was emanating through her, or the tightening in her throat as she tried to force words through its arid interior.

Felix ushered her through the throng of people, simply stating that it was a new relationship and that questions would be answered at another time.

"You okay?" His eyes held concern, like he was genuinely shocked at her turning into a mute.

"I just need a minute; the media took me by surprise."

"Sorry. I should have warned you what it would be like."

Awkward silence danced between them before Eva found herself muffling a giggle at his choice of words. Was he referring to the media onslaught, or his kiss? A part of her was a little annoyed at Felix and his high-handed decision to just kiss her and not have her agree to it beforehand.

"Don't take this the wrong way, but this is all a bit much for me to take in." She fished into her bag and pulled out a tissue, giving in to the desire to wipe away the feel of his lips against hers.

His burst of laughter was a welcome break. "I see I don't need to worry about you secretly falling for me during our ruse?" His eyes held mischief.

Glancing at the tissue, she had the good grace to look sheepish. They'd agreed their deal was 100 percent platonic, but still, having someone rub away at their lips with a tissue after a kiss was probably disheartening.

"Sorry ... I mean, it's not that you're a bad kisser ... it's just ..." She left her words hanging, trying her best not to cringe. *Way to go, Eva. Offend the man you're pretending to date.*

"Like kissing a sibling?"

"Well, I don't have siblings, but if by that you mean zero chemistry and just kind of wrong, well then, yes. It felt like that."

"If it's any consolation, it was the same for me too."

Thank goodness!

"C'mon, Miss Eva James, let's find you a drink. We can discuss better ways of handling media questions tomorrow. But for now, let's just relax and be friends. Deal?"

Now there was a plan she could get behind. "Deal."

The space was dimly lit, with soft jazz music in the air. Eva couldn't help her gaze rising to where chandeliers hung, their arms strutting at odd angles, dripping with Swarovski crystals and pendant lights. Paintings of cupids frolicking in clouds competed with ornate ceiling cornices. Rich burgundy drapes fell from arched windows. During the day, the sunlight filtering through the stained glass would be beautiful, Eva was sure.

"This is some club," Eva murmured the words, not really expecting a reply.

Booth-style tables were scattered about creating private nooks visible from the dais she and Felix stood on. The raised entrance was clever, like a stage, allowing newcomers to see and be seen. The thought that she was on show sat heavy, though she knew it was what she'd signed up for. *This wouldn't be so bad if a different prince stood beside her.* She swiped the thought away.

Tuxedo-clad waitstaff attended tables, mixing cocktails right in front of the patrons; no self-service bar for this group. Looking closer, she could see the tables were in fact fish tanks with glass tops. First the limo, then the media mobbing, now this? She felt like she'd entered another dimension. Trying to hide her unfamiliarity with such circumstances, she instead busied her fingers, massaging each one to distract herself from the rush of thoughts that she didn't belong.

"There they are, over in our corner spot. Let's go."

Each step Eva took, her stomach quivered further, tying itself in impossible knots. What would Henrik think of her kissing Felix? Would he even care? Not that she'd kissed Felix back, but Henrik wouldn't know that. She should have realised that posing as Felix's girlfriend would involve public displays of affection.

She tried not to stumble as she preceded Felix to the table, each step causing her legs to further resemble jelly. Part of her wished she was back home, keeping Gramps company as she finished some hand stitching. The other part, the part that housed her traitorous heart, was thrilled to be given the opportunity to even breathe the same air as Henrik.

She wondered again if she should have said something in the limo. He'd paused after Izzie had hopped out, had looked like he was going to put a hand up to stop her leaving, or had she imagined that? What could she have said anyway? *Hey, don't you remember me? The woman whose heart you stole five years ago when you walked away without a word and neglected to mention you're part of a royal family?*

Perhaps that was what he'd been going to tell her on their last night in Italy. He'd looked so serious when he'd said the following evening would be his last in Vernazza. Except those had been their last words, since he'd never showed up.

A hand at her waist stilled her movements. She really needed to pay more attention to the present. Dallying in the past would do nothing for her current situation.

Izzie and Sophia sat toward the middle; another unknown glamazon flanked Izzie's right side, she turned to Eva with a bored glance, her eyes narrowing a little. Henrik was sitting next to Sophia, but shifted to stand beside Eva, his arm gesturing for her to slide in to join the ladies. His good manners hadn't dwindled.

Her body tensed as she brushed past him, the hairs on

her arms reaching as if to cling to the soft wool of his suit jacket. The leather of the seat was somehow comforting, knowing he'd just been sitting there.

She'd assumed that Felix would follow her to sit at her side, so was surprised when he chose to sit next to the unknown woman, leaving Henrik to sit beside her. Anxious didn't begin to explain how she felt as his masculine smell permeated her proximity. She was momentarily thankful for the unknown woman's presence, right up until the moment her vixen glare turned in Eva's direction.

"Felix, don't tell me you bought the tailor everyone's been tweeting about? Isn't dating the hired help even below your standard?"

Ouch. Eva tried not to wince at the cattiness emanating her way. She had no clue who this woman was, but she was pretty sure they wouldn't be friends.

Izzie opened her mouth to speak.

"Harriet. Don't be a bitch." Henrik beat her to the punch.

His command brooked no discussion. And a command it certainly was. It was the first time Eva had witnessed him assert his royal position, making the gap between them run farther than the River Thames.

She'd had her fair share of critical looks, being a woman in a typically male-dominated profession, but she'd learnt the best way to take criticism was to remain silent. Let her work speak for itself. Not that the same situation applied here. She was seated opposite the 'work' she was meant to be doing.

Izzie shot Harriet a droll look. "C'mon Harriet, don't be a spoilsport. Eva is a darling and wait until you see her designs. Just keep your hands off; she'll be too busy with my outfit for the ball. She won't have time to make one for you too."

This was news to Eva. Apparently, Izzie's earlier look at Eva's sketchbook had transpired into a fully-fledged plan for a ballgown. Not that Eva was complaining. It was a dream come true to design a gown to be worn by royalty.

Eva sat back, remaining quiet as she struggled to work out if Izzie and Harriet were friends or frenemies. Usually, she was quite good at reading people; this bunch was proving well out of her league. She guessed having any kind of royal lineage would make friendships difficult, never knowing if someone was being friends to use your position and money or because they genuinely liked you. Though the same could be said for anyone dripping in wealth.

Sipping the champagne that had been passed her way, she wrinkled her nose as the bubbles burst, sprinkling her with their enthusiasm. Flicking a glance in Harriet's direction she was intrigued to see the other woman was staring at Henrik. This was the second time she'd caught her focusing Henrik's way, and the looks themselves were a little telling— overlong and with intense interest. He didn't appear to notice.

She let the other's conversation float by her, their speculation on the relationship of people she didn't know wasn't anything she could comment on either way. Other than his one sentence, Henrik appeared to have also settled into mute silence. Should she make conversation with him? But what did one talk about with a future king? *Do you wear a cape for coronation? What fabric is it made from? Do you need a tailor for the occasion?* Tongue-tied didn't come close to how she felt, adding another layer to her already bruised heart. Their time in Italy had been filled with conversation and she'd felt completely at ease. Now he seemed an entirely different person.

Clasping the glass, she took a gulp this time, trying not to choke as the bubbles danced down her throat.

"Careful." The word was a caress at her ear.

She didn't think she'd ever hear him whisper to her again, and certainly not the same word from their first meeting. His tone was silky, and she just wanted to wrap herself in its satin lengths. Had he too been remembering their time? This not knowing his thoughts or how to act was killing her.

He cleared his throat quietly, capturing her attention. She took a breath before turning, offering a tight smile which he didn't return. The goosebumps on her arms had returned, his smell and close proximity causing havoc.

"You need to take care with my brother, Miss James. He's charming to be sure, but he's not known for staying the long run, if you understand my meaning."

Honestly? She clicked her tongue, trying to contain the emotions swirling through her.

"Unlike you, right, *Your Highness*?" Looking directly into his eyes she knew the moment her words registered, his lids crushing shut. Momentary regret flashed across his features before he looked away.

Conversation continued to flow around them, the others seemingly oblivious to the turmoil Eva was experiencing. She'd agreed to this hare-brained idea of Felix's purely to help ease her financial strain, but the longer she sat in this lush leather seat, drank in the smell of the man next to her, she realised she was well out of her depth. What did it matter why he'd walked away from her? He was engaged to someone else and she knew she couldn't compete with the likes of Lady Sophia.

"Excuse me." She blurted the words, before escaping past Henrik.

Get a hold of yourself, Eva. Someone who was being paid as Felix's girlfriend shouldn't be behaving remotely like this.

Henrik resumed his seat, refusing to let his gaze follow Eva's pert behind as it rushed off. She'd been angered by his comments about taking care with Felix. Well, that made two of them. He was certainly angry at the situation himself. Why had Felix suddenly decided to deviate from his usual string of celebrities and socialites?

Glaring at his brother, he noted Harriet had left the table too, and good riddance. He didn't understand why his younger sister persisted with that friendship.

The napkin under his tumbler was sodden. The amber liquid wasn't giving him the answers he wanted, nor numbing the pain of seeing Eva's lips crushed against his brother's. He lifted his glass, peeling off the napkin before taking a long swallow. He resisted the urge to slam the tumbler back down, instead sliding the empty glass with its solo piece of ice into the table centre. He caught their waiter's eye; at least it would only be a short wait before he'd have a fresh drink.

"So, Henrik, what do you think of Eva? Do you think this will get Father off my back about being irresponsible?"

Izzie smacked Felix on the arm. "Are you only dating Eva to get off Dad's radar? Because you'd better not be! She seems sweet and lovely and a darn sight nicer than some of your previous girlfriends. She's also incredibly talented, and if you dump her before the ball, I'll have to castrate you."

"Sheesh, sis. Sometimes you're scary."

"Not as scary as I'll be if I lose to Harriet on Vogue's best-dressed lists after the royal ball. Or next week's garden party.

Do you think Eva would be keen to make me something for that?"

Henrik stood, unable to listen to them any longer. He should ask Sophia to dance, or check whether she needed another drink, but he couldn't be bothered. Right now, he couldn't bring himself to be the royal crown prince, or the soon-to-be-engaged man, or even her friend. He needed to find some air.

Spotting the wooden doors, he headed towards the back entrance for some peace and quiet.

The club lighting was dim, filled with buzzing conversation interspersed with occasional loud laughter. The music floated in and out of his consciousness, making him aware it was there but not enough for him to pay attention to the name of the song. His bodyguards would be hanging around the edge of the premises, having checked the list of everyone inside the club. It was one of the bonuses of coming here— he could have slightly more freedom from their presence.

He pushed through the heavy oak door, feeling lighter as it shut behind him, muting a lot of the noise and buzzing in his head. His leather shoes tapped against the polished concrete floor, echoing slightly as he reached the end of the corridor.

The ladies' bathroom door opened just as he reached for the handle that would lead him outside. Eva halted when she spotted him, surprise evident on her face. He took another step, clasping the handle, a questioning brow raised towards her.

"Would you care to join me for some air?" Never before had he felt he'd spoken such a loaded question. Her presence was making him feel and act foolish. Seconds ticked by as he waited to see what she'd do.

Eva said nothing as she slipped past him into the crisp night air, taking a few steps into the small garden area. "Why did you pretend we'd never met?"

Delicious smells from a restaurant next door accompanied the perfume that lingered after Eva. She shivered, and he could see her arms prickle in the cold air. On autopilot, he shrugged off his jacket. Moving to stand before her, he draped it across her shoulders, its tailored lines swamping her petite form.

"Thank you. Why, Henrik?"

He'd heard her question but was struggling to find the words to answer it. The sound of his name on her lips was like coming home after years away. Why had he pretended they'd never met? Part of him had worried that owning up to a connection to her would make his brother more interested. Though it appeared that had been a futile worry, since she was dating his brother anyway.

"Were you dating my brother in London?"

A small sound of annoyance emitted from those delicious lips. She'd been staring at him, but at his words she moved to study the ground at her feet. "How is that any of your business? Look, just forget I asked."

"He's my brother, I think that makes it my business."

"Seriously? Fine. No, I wasn't dating your brother in London, we'd only just met. I've answered your question, I think it's time you answer mine."

They weren't dating last week? Then whatever they are must be very new ... Which makes Felix having brought her here to his country, so soon, rather unusual.

"I'm sorry I didn't acknowledge you in London."

Eva dropped her head back, her breath huffing out. "I didn't ask for an apology, Henrik. I asked why? *Why* did you ignore me? *Why* did you never show up all those years ago in Italy? You do remember me, don't you?"

Her last question was posed as an afterthought, her face a picture of confusion, her voice stilted. He wanted to take her in his arms and kiss away all her worries. But he couldn't do that. He waited, buying himself time, but he couldn't lie to her. Of course he remembered her. He remembered every second of their short time together.

"Yes, I remember you."

She stared at him, clearly waiting for him to continue. He remained mute.

After a moment she shook her head as if to clear it, her eyes imploring him for answers that wouldn't help either of them. "I thought we had a connection all those years ago in Italy, but it seems I'm the only one. I clearly never knew you at all."

Her words hit him like a physical blow and although his instinct for self-restraint and self-preservation roared at him to remember his role, remember her apparent relationship with his brother, his heart took control. He couldn't hold back anymore. Having her this close, looking at him with those molten chocolate eyes, he needed to know if their connection was still as strong. He needed to hold her. To taste her.

"To hell with it."

Her eyes flicked up as he closed the gap between them. Her dark-rimmed lashes fluttered before understanding took over, and her lids floated closed as his mouth captured hers in a gentle caress. He drank in her taste, the dryness of the champagne a stark contrast to her sweet lips.

He stroked his tongue along her bottom lip, requesting permission as she opened to him. He'd told himself he needed air, but it'd been a lie. He'd needed her. Memories tumbled one after another as his body hardened, desperate to feel her skin against his.

Only their lips touched, but it wasn't enough, his hands finding her hips, guiding her closer to him. His thumb stroked the silk at her back, knowing the skin beneath was smoother, wanting that caress. Her fingers found his arms, gripping tighter as the kiss deepened. A slight moan against his mouth had him wishing they were somewhere more private.

He broke away. Shallow breaths sounded between them, heat and longing so quick to spring to life, just like it had previously. The passion she'd evoked in him hadn't dissipated, and he needed it to.

Cupping her face, he placed one last kiss at her temple before shutting his eyes. He ground out his parting words.

"Damn you, Eva. Go home."

6

*E*va placed another stitch in the hessian pad, cross-stitching over others to stabilise the structure. Deep breath in, stitch, deep breath out. The razor-sharp point of her needle nicked her finger, drawing a small drop of blood. Cursing her stupidity, and lack of concentration on the job, she dumped the sewing to search for a Band-Aid.

He'd kissed her.

The pesky little sentence blew into her mind yet again. Just like it had constantly for the past twenty-four hours. Why had he kissed her? Maybe it had been an apology ... yet if that had been the case, he wouldn't have told her to go home ... would he? Also, since when had kissing become a form of apology? Gah! She was driving herself insane.

At least she finally had some work to do. Felix had mentioned a royal garden party event last night, to be held the following week. Eva had jumped at the chance of doing some work—even tailoring work. He'd initially laughed at her suggestion but then must have noticed the look of desperation in her eyes. She needed something to do and this was the perfect answer, plus it would mean more coverage for James Tailoring. Just because she wasn't working in the atelier in London didn't mean she couldn't attribute the work to her gramps' business.

Plus, this made her feel better about the fact she was taking payment from Felix. So far, she felt like a fraud on the pretend girlfriend part. She was pretty sure kissing his brother hadn't been part of the deal ... and there her thoughts went again. Back to the kiss. Should she tell Felix about her interlude with Henrik? Maybe she should admit to him that they have a past ... Not telling him only added to her feelings of inadequacy for the role she was being paid for.

Having dealt with her finger, she dragged herself out of the chair, moving to the mannequin to check the fit of the jacket. Her Gramps had been so proud on the phone this morning, excited and honoured by the article she'd read out to him from the local paper. It had been a glowing piece about James Tailoring, and Eva hoped it would send more business their way. Felix was really holding up his end of the deal, which didn't help the guilt Eva was struggling to pull herself out of. She made a mental note to speak to Felix, see if there was anything else she could do to help with this 'avaricious ex' of his. She'd been surprised the mystery woman hadn't made an appearance last night, unless it was Harriet?

Or maybe it was someone else who had turned up, but Eva had been outside, kissing Henrik. Which brought her thoughts back around in a circle again, still no clearer on a reason for Henrik kissing her. More than anything she longed for someone to talk to about this. She had friends back home, but no one she felt she could confide in. Gramps was her only family, but he wasn't the right person for this type of conversation either. Her mum would be a perfect person to call except she'd been taken from Eva's life at a young age.

Eva's heart ached even more. She wished she could just jump on a plane and go home, hide from this whole ordeal, but the stronger side of her, the side that had enabled her to slowly but surely recover from Henrik's Italian disappearing act, hardened her heart. She'd already been here a week; only three more to go. Then she could return home, money in hand, and focus again on putting a smile back on her gramps' face. Simple, right?

She sighed, sinking back down into the chair. Why the hell did she have to go around complicating things by kissing a liar from the past—even if he was a crown prince?

Henrik slammed the newspaper down on Felix's lap, resisting the urge to go wash his hands. Felix choked on the sip of coffee he'd been midway through when his lap had taken a beating.

"Have you spoken to Miss James about this, Felix?"

Felix casually lean forward, placing his cup back on the coffee tray before slowly folding out the paper. Henrik itched to snatch it back and fold it out himself, shove it in Felix's face, then bin the offending piece.

Felix scanned the article, breaking into a smile before folding it neatly and placing it back on his lap.

"Why do I need to speak to her? It's a glowing review of her grandfather's tailoring atelier in London—it's probably going to help send business her way. Other than a small mention of our acquaintance, I don't see that it's in any way negative."

That was it? Henrik paused, mentally berating his foolishness for not reading the article before storming off to find his brother. Stefan had handed him the paper after his breakfast meeting with the museum board. The front-page image of Felix and Eva smiling for the camera, Eva's face locked in a fake smile, had ice filling his veins. It was one thing for his brother to date Eva, but seeing her splashed across the main Geravia tabloid was sending his head spinning.

"Actually, brother, if you're worried about Eva you should go see her. I've got a few meetings I can't get out of today, and she said she had itchy fingers for work. Perhaps you could update your wardrobe whilst you were at it?"

Felix's face was carefully innocent. It was driving Henrik mad that he couldn't interpret Felix's end game. When the brothers were younger, they'd often engaged in strategic mind games—preparation for royal life, they'd called it. They'd driven their sister crazy with them, their mother the only one who'd seemed to understand ... but that was years ago ... before ...

Henrik shook off that thought. He needed to speak to Eva either way, apologise about last night. Perhaps under the pretence of work, she'd be more willing to speak to him.

Leaving without giving his brother an answer, Henrik headed for the guest suites at the other end of the palace. Inside the palace was one of the few places he could walk unaccompanied by bodyguards. He knew they watched him on camera and lingered out of sight at strategic points throughout the castle. His father was more closely guarded than he, even inside, so Henrik's freedom wouldn't last forever, but at times like now it made life easier. The walls of the palace were beautiful, filled with prestigious artworks and family heirlooms that had been added to the Stenish royal family over centuries.

He should feel lucky he lived in such luxury, had been born to such privilege. But these past few years, he'd been feeling more and more like the lavish walls were forming a prison.

Henrik paused before entering Eva's half open door, there wasn't much he was afraid of but facing Eva after his behaviour last night, scared the heck out of him. *Here went nothing.* He walked in unannounced, reluctant to offer her an opportunity to shut him out before he got to say anything.

He was surprised to see her weaving a figure eight, contemplating the carpet. His heart slowed, time stilling as he watched her walk. She'd often just wandered about in circles or other shapes when deep in thought. He should be surprised by how easily memories of her came back to him after such a time, but it seemed they were heavily ingrained. Just what was occupying her mind now?

She was dressed casually, slim pants that hugged her long legs, topped off with a thick jumper. She'd left her hair loose, her face bare of makeup. She looked vulnerable somehow, a small frown knitting her eyebrows together. Her hair was shorter than it had been in Italy. Her eyes held a little less sparkle.

A part of his heart urged him to walk to her, take her into his arms and never let go. But a bigger part shut the thought down. He would test the waters, employ her 'itchy fingers' for work, as Felix put it, then he'd apologise for the kiss. And then he'd walk away.

"Is the carpet that fascinating?" She jumped like a cat

sprayed with water. All thoughts of composure and professionalism flew out the window. *What is he doing here?*

His face was a calm mask, like those she'd spent too much time poring over on the internet recently. She tried to remind her body he was seeing someone else. That the kiss hadn't meant anything. But it seemed she was deceiving herself. It was going to take more than countless hours of telling herself to move on. Her body wasn't getting the memo. She focused her gaze on the ground, hoping that by not seeing him she'd be less affected. Perhaps she could pretend he wasn't really in the room? *Perhaps there are pigs flying outside.*

"I'm here for a fitting."

"I'm sorry?" Confusion laced her words, evidence of the disconnect between mind and body.

"You asked what I was doing here."

She had? Flicking a quick glance back to his face she caught the slight smile creeping across his otherwise blank face, his humour at her confusion making her angry. "I did not!"

"You said, and I quote, 'What is he doing here?'"

I must have spoken my thoughts out loud. Not only is he driving my body mad by his presence, he's driving my mind mad too.

"My apologies. *Your Highness.*" The last she said as an afterthought.

She pointed to the dais that squatted next to the mannequin. Fitting Henrik a suit was one of the last things she wanted to do. But she couldn't exactly say no. "If you please, I'll try and be brief, Your Highness."

"Call me Henrik." His voice softened.

Eva shut her eyes at his tone. How easy it was to remember the different Henrik, the one she'd met in Italy, when he spoke softly. When she could imagine a smile lighting up his face in a carefree manner. Not trusting her voice to answer, she offered a short nod.

"Do I need to remove any clothes?"

"No!" her voice was shrill. *Goodness, had he read her mind?*

"I can just do the measurements over what you are wearing." Mental pep talk finished, she looked at his body properly for the first time and realised her mistake. "Oh ..." Her mouth stayed in a slack *O* as her voice drifted off.

He was dressed for the depths of the arctic in a bulky Aran sweater that looked soft and inviting. Her hands twitched. Jeans clung to his strong thighs. She'd seen him dressed formally, which had taken her breath away. But something about seeing him in casual clothing clutched at her heart. She was transported back to the original Henrik she'd met. The approachable Henrik. She really needed to find a way to remove those memories.

Twirling the tape measure around her wrist, she tried to appear composed. Taking measurements over that outfit was not going to work.

"I'm guessing you'd like to re-consider those instructions?"

Damn him, was he enjoying her discomfort? What else would explain that odd look on his face?

"Hmm." Not quite meeting his eyes, she fluttered her hand as a signal of agreement. Taking refuge behind the design desk, she waited an appropriate amount of time for him to shed his jumper. Flashes in her peripheral suggested he was done and waiting. Taking a fortifying breath, she stood, wiping her suddenly sweaty hands across her thighs.

Oh lordy. This was going to test her willpower.

He was standing on the dais. Ramrod straight, and utterly uncovered to the low-slung waist of his jeans. She wanted to ask him to pose like David just for the added thrill. Her mouth watered at the bare flesh on show.

He hadn't changed much since she'd last seen him so deliciously undressed. He was perhaps a touch leaner, but his muscles had in no way diminished. He lifted a hand to run it through his hair, the muscles in his forearm cording at the movement. Could he hear her heart beating a tattoo in her chest? If he asked it would probably just jump right out into his hand, such was the effect he had on her. Had always had on her.

It was that thought that shocked her out of her trance. He'd met her, wined, dined and ravished her. And lied to her. Yet she still wanted him. What did that say about her? It made her feel weak and annoyed beyond belief. Added to that, he'd then pretended not to know her, then kissed her last night after it must have been clear she was 'dating' Felix and when he was supposed to have a fiancée?. *Urgh.* Thinking about the situation she'd managed to get herself into was starting to hurt her brain.

Setting her features, she stamped forward, whipping the tape measure from her neck. She was a professional. So, he was partially naked. So what? She'd measured plenty of men in similar stages of undress.

"You're angry with me." The words were matter of fact; his tone gave nothing away.

"What on earth gives you that idea?" Sarcasm dripped like honey from her words.

"The narrowing of your brows was the initial giveaway. But you've also just pursed your lips. That was the clincher."

How dare he! He was the one who'd kissed her last night! She wasn't sure what he hoped to achieve from his words. His face had remained passive throughout. Eva was struggling with this new Henrik. He seemed so lifeless.

"Sorry." It was the first word he'd said that held any variation in tone. The soft murmur left Eva seething even more, particularly as it was the first time he'd sounded like the old Henrik, the one from her dreams.

"That's it. You're sorry?"

"I'm not sure what you're looking for here, Eva."

"I'm not looking for anything. I just want you to acknowledge that you remember me. Clearly our week in Italy meant different things to me than it did you, but that doesn't excuse you to act like a ... a ... wanker!" The word ripped out. Mortified, she clapped a hand over her runaway mouth. She'd just called a crown prince a wanker. So much for keeping her feelings hidden and remaining professional.

"I can say sorry again if you'd like." His face was a mask, but he wouldn't meet her eyes.

How did she get this so wrong? She hadn't been going to say anything. She'd just do her job, take the money, and leave. But being alone with him now ... it had just started spilling out.

Their week together had been everything to her. It was the first time she'd ever really connected with a man. Sure, she'd had boyfriends, but something had always been missing. Until Henrik. Her body could still remember the tingle from their first contact, her heart still ached to feel that connection to him once more. Had she just imagined their love?

"Eva, I really am sorry. It was wrong of me to pretend I didn't know you in London, and it was wrong that I never showed in Italy. But I had my reasons. I'm also sorry I kissed you last night; it won't happen again. It's better this way."

His words hit home. *Better for whom?* "Well, that's a new twist on the whole 'it's not you, it's me' line. Do you just pop over to Italy whenever you're bored, looking for a new conquest?"

Something akin to hurt flashed on his face before the stone wall reappeared, his jaw tightened and set. She'd probably imagined the softening. Nothing about Henrik was soft. Not this Henrik anyway. She could almost see the invisible but somehow tangible crown that sat atop his head. Every inch the king-to-be.

Turning away after her parting shot, she looped her measuring tape about her neck. The familiar gesture offered comfort.

"I'm sorry."

"Stop saying sorry! I don't want your pity," she snapped in despair. Her hands tossed at the air, asking for an answer to the impossible situation she'd gotten herself into.

"Then what do you want?" Two long strides had him pinning her against the desk. A glimpse of the old Henrik who showed emotion was back, his eyes darkening as they captured hers. His actions robbed her of speech.

Heavy breaths were the only sound to break the silence.

The word 'you' wanted to escape but instead she uttered the sensible option.

"I want your in-seam measurement."

It diffused the situation instantly. His short laugh floated at her ear, scattering goosebumps in its wake. *Oh that sound,* her eyes closed briefly in weakness.

"It's one hundred and five centimetres. I had Stefan collect my measurements from my tailor. I thought it might make this less ..." He shrugged instead of finishing his sentence. Pulling a folded piece of paper with scribbled numbers from his pocket, he handed it over.

"If you had these all along, why did you come?"

For a long while she wasn't sure she was going to get an

answer. She watched as he methodically buttoned a crisp white shirt, then shrugged into his chunky knit.

"Well?"

"Well what?" His eyes met hers briefly before flicking away. Was that pain she'd seen there, or her imagination?

"Aren't you going to answer?"

He walked to the door and pulled it toward him before turning to her one last time. "You said to stop saying sorry."

The door closed with his parting words.

A sense of disappointment flashed through her. He'd apologised. Except there was no reasoning for his actions. That was what she really wanted, deep down. Needed. But his apology seemed to have closed the book on that front.

She pulled on the tape around her neck until it cut into her skin, physical pain to distract from the emotional pain, and shook her head. He was a taken man, and she needed to stick with her decision from this morning. Time to put him out of her mind.

7

Eva shrugged her shoulder, shifting the silk fabric that clung there a fraction higher. The fit of the dress was immaculate. She should know; she'd spent hours perfecting it with a little help from one of the seamstresses often contracted to help at the palace. It had been a godsend that she'd turned up; self-fitting was a hard and tireless job.

"Thanks for sending Mabel. She was lovely and a wondrous help." Eva gave Felix's arm a little squeeze as she said the words. She was equal parts excited and nervous. Excited to be stepping out in one of her designs; nervous about others, including members of the media, seeing it. And a certain someone. Dammit. Why were her thoughts always going there? His dark gaze never seemed to leave her thoughts. Whenever she closed her eyes, he was there, waiting. A dream that was never going to be a reality.

"Who's Mabel?" Felix turned a quizzical brow her way.

"The seamstress? You sent her to help me fit this dress."

"Which, I haven't yet told you, is stunning. A fact you're talented enough to know yourself. The media will be gobbling up your pictures. I don't know any seamstresses though."

The last he seemed to say as an afterthought before stopping to greet a group of people on the outskirts of the lawn. Eva was drawn to his side, smiling and returning offered hands for shaking or cheeks for kissing. All the while, her thoughts were distracted. If Felix hadn't sent Mabel, then who the hell had?

A tug at her arm, closely followed by an exuberant hug and a waft of gardenia, told her Izzie had arrived.

"Eva, you look gorgeous! I want that dress." Izzie pouted as she looked down at her own dress.

"I can arrange for one to be made for you. Mabel helped me with this; I'm sure she could help me make another for you in between helping with your ballgown."

"Mabel?"

"The seamstress. Oh, I should have realised it was you who sent her! To help me make your ballgown?"

Izzie's tinkling laugh floated in the air. "Eva, I've no idea what you're on about, but anything that helps make my dress fabulous is fine by me."

Hmm, okay, that was odd. If it wasn't Felix or Izzie who arranged the help for Eva, then who had it been?

She pushed the thought aside. She needed to focus on today—focus on not making a fool of herself.

The back of her neck prickled, and she started to turn before she could stop herself. Henrik must have been close by. A quick scan didn't reveal him though. She huffed a little frustrated sigh at herself.

"Is my company that boring?" Felix's voice held amusement.

Eva had forgotten he was even there. So much for playing the doting girlfriend.

"Sorry, no, of course not." She shifted closer, leaning her head in towards his, like she had seen other couples do.

He let out a quiet snort then whispered in her ear. "Eva, you could never be an actress. I've seen pillows look at me more lovingly than you have."

"Felix. Miss James."

Henrik's voice rolled over her like a silky caress. She'd sensed he was nearby, but her heart still skipped when he moved into view. Sophia stood by his side, her arm casually linked through his. He stood ramrod straight, like he was being fitted for the suit he wore. A suit she'd tailored for him. She couldn't fault her work, and her treacherous heart gleamed with pride knowing her work sat against his skin, enhancing his powerful body.

Eva stashed away the envy she felt seeing Sophia next to Henrik. "Sophia, you look beautiful."

"Speak for yourself! You really must let me introduce you to some people back in London. That dress you're wearing is simply divine—we need to get your label happening whilst all this hype is flying. I can't say much for your taste in men, but it's certainly helping get your name out there."

Sophia laughed and winked at Felix. Standing glued to Felix's side, Eva felt him tense at Sophia's words. *Interesting.* Felix clearly didn't appreciate Sophia's jibe.

"Thanks Sophia. That's kind of you to say." She was saved from adding to her somewhat lame reply by the arrival of one of Sophia's friends who drew the others into conversation. Eva took the moment to calm herself.

The sky hadn't come to the party, swirling with puffy grey clouds, threatening rain at any moment. She felt silly wearing sunglasses but had to concede that right now they were helping her, allowing her to drink in the sight of

Henrik with no one being the wiser. She was failing miserably in her goal to forget him.

Since his apology she'd only seen him a handful of times. Each time he'd been polite, nothing to give her any reason to believe he had feelings for her. Yet she still couldn't shake off thoughts of their kiss. Why had he kissed her? He was engaged to Sophia. He knew she was dating Felix—fake dating, true—but he didn't know that. Or did he? Had he kissed her because he knew this thing with Felix was fake? Was that his way of warning her off?

Since the night at the club she'd been out with Felix various times, each with carefully planned locations, outfits and media opportunities. She eyed the striking figures of Henrik and Felix, knowing her work stood out. How she wished Gramps were here to see the James family tradition taking its place on the world stage. Speaking to her Gramps every so often acted as a helpful reminder for why she was putting herself through this turmoil.

She'd enjoyed reading snippets about her designs but had tried to push that pride aside to focus on what it was doing for James Tailoring.

Gramps' happiness and saving the business was what mattered.

Izzie returned to their group, this time with Harriet in tow.

Eva blinked a few times at the sight before her. Harriet's outfit bordered on indecent. They were at a royal garden party event for heaven's sake, not a strip club. The dress was white and almost translucent due to its tight nature. She heard Henrik utter a curse under his breath, a sure sign that he agreed. Overpowering fumes of Chanel N°5 reached Eva, causing her to wonder if Harriet had sprayed herself with it or showered in it.

"Harriet, what on earth are you wearing?" It was the first time Eva had heard Felix sound shocked. "You'd best go find something else. The press group will be here any minute for their allocated photos. The media will have a field day if they see you in that dress."

Too late, thought Eva, spotting a group of people sporting cameras, press passes slung around their necks. She'd been prepped for this, instructed by the communications advisor on the best way to act, what to say, and where to stand. She'd practiced how best to show off her dress which she'd spent many painstaking hours making as perfect as possible. Her other hours had been spent finishing both Felix and Henrik's suits. It had kept her fingers busy and given her something to focus on late into the evenings when sleep had been a struggle.

Henrik must have spotted the press as well because he began muttering under his breath. Eva was surprised to see him start to shrug out of his jacket, which would totally ruin the lines of his outfit. Realising he was going to offer it to Harriet, she held up a hand to stop him.

"Wait, I've a jacket she can wear." Eva had left hers with Stefan, thinking she wouldn't need it. As if reading her mind, he appeared, handing it over.

"I don't need to wear a jacket. You are such prudes. This dress is glamorous."

Eva chose not to answer—just held the jacket out towards the taller woman.

"Oh fine, I'll put it on. But it's your dress design you're covering up, Eva. I thought you'd want every inch of exposure you could get."

She spoke the words loudly, so they reached the crowd who were gathered next to Stefan. Every word would have reached them. Every. Single. One.

Fear pooled in Eva's stomach and she felt physically ill. She opened her mouth to dispute Harriet's claim but was too late. Harriet plucked the jacket from Eva's limp fingertips, twirling it up around her shoulders. She didn't bother to put it on properly, letting it drape down both arms, almost like a cape to her villainous outfit.

Words just wouldn't form at Harriet's blatant lie. In shock, she turned to Henrik, finding his eyes meeting hers in equal confusion.

Eva finally found her voice. "But—"

"Lady Harriet, can you tell us who you're wearing today? That's certainly more daring than we're used to for a crown event."

Eva squeezed her eyes shut. The sound of rushing water drowned out any response Harriet might have made. Her mind whirred like her sewing machine jammed at high speed. She couldn't think. Couldn't respond. She was unable to sort out a course of action other than stand there, a mute.

She'd walked into this situation. They were surrounded by hundreds of Stenaco's elite, with delegates from around the world—even one of the British royal family was attending. This event was huge, and she was about to take the fall for a hideous dress design all because of some woman with a bitchy agenda.

Finally, blood rushed back in, her brain clicking into motion. Henrik and Felix must have both recovered at the same time, as they both moved to take one of Harriet's arms. Eva cut them both off with a shake of her head.

Putting on her best smile, she stepped next to Harriet, trying to ignore the feeling of being a midget compared to the six-foot-tall piece of work. She had to hand it to her. Whilst the dress was distasteful, there weren't many who would be able to pull off it. Reaching up, Eva unhooked the jacket, holding it out for Harriet to put on properly. Harriet looked at her like one would a fly before meeting her steely gaze. Something in it must have made her realise Eva meant business, so after a subtle eye roll, she shrugged into the jacket.

"The jacket is by James Tailoring. I organised the outfit for Harriet as a favour but there must have been a miscommunication. I *only* designed the jacket. I can't take credit for the dress. That's all Harriet."

She said the last part with a saccharine smile thrown Harriet's way, but beneath the fake sugar of her expression, rage coursed through her. How dare this woman try and throw her under the bus? She'd only met her once, but clearly the woman had something against her.

Then it clicked. Harriet must be the ex-girlfriend Felix was referring to.

She made a mental note to confirm this later, so she'd be better prepared. It irritated her that Felix hadn't warned her that Harriet might pull a stunt like this. It hadn't occurred to her when they'd first met at the nightclub, as Harriet had barely stayed at the table, and hadn't at all acknowledged Eva other than her initial belittling comment. Eva had assumed Harriet had a thing for Henrik given it was him she'd stared at whenever she was at the table. A fact Eva only noted as she'd been doing the same.

"Well, well, well. The kitten has claws."

The spiteful words were whispered in Eva's ear so only she would hear them. She assumed Harriet had been hoping to throw her off guard again, but it had the opposite effect. It gave Eva strength. She wouldn't be bullied by some random woman in front of the media. This meant too much to her.

She caught Henrik's eye as he moved to stand before the

press, addressing them directly and effectively blocking any further images of Eva and Harriet. His gaze was assessing. Almost worried?

Felix's hand sliding around her waist and guiding her away gave her space to breathe.

"Well, you just saved that potential debacle for yourself. Well done. You're a natural in front of the media. Nerves of steel. I'm seriously impressed. Not many people would have handled that with such aplomb."

Eva wasn't sure it had anything to do with aplomb, but she was thankful she'd managed to get out of it unscathed. There was no way she wanted to get caught being accredited for someone else's lewd designs. That sort of negative press would be terrible for her Gramps.

"I'm glad you think so. But now would be a good time for you to own up to why Harriet doesn't like me. She's the ex, isn't she?"

She narrowed her eyes at Felix, looking for any signs of evasion like she'd received previously when she'd asked about the mysterious ex. Before today, she'd been starting to wonder if Felix had made it up.

Felix grimaced, then looked away. It wasn't a verbal confirmation, but Eva had to assume it was the only one she'd receive given he appeared to get lost looking at something else over Eva's shoulder. He patted her arm, almost a fatherly move.

"Sorry about Harriet. She's been faux friends with Izzie since they met at finishing school. I'm never sure if Izzie even really likes her or keeps her around because she feels sorry for her. Which sounds terrible, but Harriet isn't the sort you want to get on the bad side of. Plus, her dad is one of the richest men in Stenaco and has a fairly large influence with our government. The political association makes cutting ties hard."

Eva soaked in Felix's words. That explained a lot. Not why Harriet chose to target her perhaps, but it explained why she felt she could swan around like she belonged at the palace.

The same prickling sensation from earlier ran up Eva's spine. Turning, she caught sight of Henrik walking their way. He looked so regal, delicious to the point Eva hoped drool didn't slide out the corner of her mouth. Jet black hair curled slightly around his ears. Her fingers tingled at the thought of running them through it. The suit she'd laboured on through the quiet hours of the night sat elegantly across his shoulders, emphasising their strength and breadth. What was the saying? The suit maketh the man? Not in this case. Eva was pretty sure she could have tailored a sack and Henrik would still look powerful striding across the lawn. Powerful and unattainable.

Her body betrayed her stern instructions to cut all emotional reactions to him. Heat swept up her neck and she knew the carefully applied rouge was unnecessary on her cheeks. Hopefully Henrik would be too much of a gentleman to comment.

She closed her eyes before they travelled any farther south. Her mind didn't need more fodder for those thoughts.

"Felix, Father is searching for you. I'll keep Miss James company until you can return."

Equal parts joy and despair shot through Eva as she watched Felix walk away in search of the King. Her panicked look did not go unnoticed by her new companion. Stealing herself, she turned to him, determined to offer him an excuse to leave her alone.

"I don't want to impose. I'm sure Lady Sophia is looking for you."

"So quick to dismiss me, Eva?" Henrik's tone held an edge that Eva couldn't interpret.

"I was offering you a polite excuse to leave. It's something you do well."

The words were out before she could call them back. Feelings she'd been trying to keep hidden bubbled to the surface, frustration amongst them. She still wanted a proper explanation, no matter how many lectures she gave herself to just move on.

Henrik nodded, seemingly unsurprised at her words. "I wanted to check that you're okay? After the press photos?"

"You mean after Harriet tried to make me look like a fool?"

His lips flattened to a straight line. "Yes, that. I've spoken to Harriet, informed her any repeat conduct of that nature will not be tolerated." He turned to face her directly. "I'm sorry she did that. You handled yourself really well."

Eva raised a brow at the support from Henrik, unsure of the concern that seemed to lie beneath his words.

"Thank you ..."

He pocketed his hands, still looking directly at her face. His scrutiny was making her nervous. "I didn't get to finish my apology the other day. Please accept it now. I'm sorry for pretending I didn't know you in London. It was wrong of me."

"Why did you?"

Eva could barely breath, desperately willing him to answer her question. She wasn't sure she was going to get a response; the pause was so great.

"I was in shock. You were the last person I was expecting to see with my brother."

She swallowed to bring moisture to her arid dry mouth. "I see." Eva wasn't sure what she'd been hoping for. Clearly it wasn't going to be any form of love declaration.

"I don't think you do. Eva ... our week in Italy, it was a fantasy life for me. This is my real life."

And you don't belong here. Henrik didn't need to say those words. Eva knew his meaning from the pained expression on his face.

"Well, thank you for the clarification. In any case, it's in the past. I'm very happy with Felix." Each word Eva spoke drove the knife in a little harder. She only hoped Henrik was buying her lies.

Henrik's eyes went three shades darker. "You should take care with Felix. He's fickle with women."

She remained silent. Henrik had confirmed her own thoughts from the moment she found out who he really was. He was royalty. She was a nobody. She didn't belong in his world.

"So you've said before."

Eva spotted Izzie beckoning her, and excusing herself, she took the chance to run, not bothering to wait for any answer from Henrik. Walking away, she desperately wished for home. First thing tomorrow morning she'd call her Gramps to check in.

Hearing his voice would help renew her resolve for this job.

---

8

*H*enrik looked around at the Garden party, seeing an array of smiling faces and an abundant consumption of champagne. Just another royal event, except this time he couldn't even pretend he was enjoying himself.

How did he fix these feelings churning inside him? This morning's paper had been bad enough. More images of Eva and Felix splashed across the pages, the royals new favourite duo. Jealousy had coursed through him like a black cloud.

He needed to let this go. Eva wasn't an option for him. He'd agreed to marry Sophia; she was the best option for his path in life. Eva had only been here a short time and already his life was turned upside down, searching media articles, assigning seamstresses. His carefully constructed focus was falling to pieces having her so close. This feeling of being unable to control his emotions was spreading through him like a virus. He needed to take a break before he did something crazy like declare his true feelings for Eva to Felix and beg his brother to send her back home.

Eva was still in his line of sight, standing with his sister and Sophia, the three making a stunning picture, all poise and fashionable figures at the garden party. He was surprised by how relaxed she looked, how well she fit. He'd chosen to stay standing just apart from the crowd, taking a precious moment to himself before going back into the fray. He knew it wasn't acceptable for him to ignore palace guests, but he'd wanted to ensure she really was okay after the earlier press debacle.

He'd dressed this morning, worry lacing his fingers as he'd struggled to put buttons through buttonholes Eva herself had sewn, his gut churning over how she'd cope with today. He had made sure she'd received all available media training and preparation, advised Stefan to keep a close eye on her. He needn't have worried. She was a picture of calm, had handled the Harriet situation skilfully in front of the press.

The dress she wore made her look like a beautiful goddess, strips of fabric running in various directions, intricately pieced together. The skirt floated to just below the knee, hitting all the correct notes for being fashionable yet appropriate for such an event. Appropriate? Who was he kidding? Appropriate for every other red-blooded male at the function, perhaps. But not for him, all he could think about was peeling her out of it, inch by well-stitched inch.

Get a grip, he admonished himself.

His body tensed at the sight of Harriet joining Eva's group. Why was she still here? He'd told her to leave! Taking a determined step forward to reiterate his request, his pace quickened at the evil grin he saw on Harriet's face.

As if in slow motion, Eva shifted slightly to the side, her heel catching on something before she started to tumble backwards. The skirt of her dress floated. Time slowed as he realised where she was falling.

"Oh shit."

Heart racing, he rushed forward, the splash of water followed by various levels of gasps and concern. It was a such a stupid idea to have a water feature on the lawn, especially with the lowest tier so low to the ground. It was the centrepiece of the area, multi-tiered with water spraying from the top, but right now it was going to give him a bloody heart attack. The media were still around; no way would Eva escape unscathed from images of her dunking in the icy pond.

She was sputtering water when he reached out to pull her to a standing position. Her eyes spat fire at the laughing figure of Harriet who stood taking pictures on her mobile. He grabbed the offending device, silencing her protests with a glare of his own.

He shoved the phone into his pocket before shrugging out of his jacket and cocooning it around Eva's shaking shoulders. The cloudy skies hid any sunshine and he imagined the water must be freezing. He drew the jacket lapels together before fitting her under his arm and marching her off the grounds.

All thoughts of propriety fled, his only focus on protecting Eva and getting her away from the crowd. How could he have been so stupid? After the press stunt, he should have made sure Harriet had followed his orders to leave. Shoving the thoughts aside to revisit later, he didn't stop to look where he was taking Eva until she emitted a small hiccup.

"Are you okay?"

"Seriously? No, I'm not okay, that … woman! How dare she? What on earth have I ever done to her?" Venom laced her tone. He was surprised by her reaction; he'd expected her to be upset.

"Harriet's a born troublemaker. I'm sorry."

His words had Eva spinning to a stop. Even drenched she was beautiful. Her whiskey eyes flashed at him. Tiny droplets of water sat on her lashes and he wished more than anything to kiss them away. He wanted to drag her back into his embrace and never let her go.

She shrugged her arms properly into the jacket, patches of water spreading across the silvery-grey front. He watched as she overlapped the right side, its size swamping her to the point it nearly reached around to her back before she anchored it in place with her crossed arms. The sound of water pitting onto the ground at their feet rang into the silence.

He looked around, seeing pristine white roses interspersed with pale pink and lilac cherry blossom blooms. His feet had taken control, taking Eva to the one place he knew they wouldn't be disturbed. He was never interrupted when he came into his mother's garden. The colour of the blooms told him they were nearly at the wisteria-filled centre of the maze. He waited for the panic to take over, the overwhelming sadness and urge to run. It was still there, but somehow it was masked from its usual level. He turned a small circle before again focusing on the dripping figure before him who looked at him in utter confusion.

"We're in the rose garden maze. Perhaps I should be the one asking you if you're okay? You've got a very strange look on your face." The corner of her lips lifted in a small smile.

"Sorry. I don't know why I brought you here. I guess I wasn't thinking." He hadn't been going to say that. He always knew what to think, was always careful to check what words passed his mouth. Though there were people he hadn't needed to do that with. It had been a while, but one of those people stood before him right now.

"This was your mother's design, wasn't it? The garden? Sophia said she loved it ... I can see why."

The words shocked him out of his spell. "We should get you inside, out of those wet clothes. I don't know why I brought you here."

Her eyebrows shot towards her hairline.

"Um." Then she giggled. The sound was a breath of fresh air to the brief emptiness he'd felt at the mention of his mother.

"Actually, if you don't mind, I might wait it out here a bit longer. Catch my breath, maybe plot revenge on Harriet." Her smile told him she was joking.

He was thankful she hadn't further commented on his request to remove her clothes. The image that flashed when he spoke those words didn't help either of them.

"Aren't you cold?" He narrowed his eyes slightly, taking in the goosebumps that rippled along her arms. She'd only been in the water a minute, but it was enough of a drenching to see her dress slicked against her legs. A puddle had formed on the pavers at her feet. He worried she'd end up catching a cold if she stayed dressed as she was.

"I'm fine, really. You should go. I wouldn't want to keep you." Her eyes darted from his as she spoke the words, and he knew he couldn't leave her.

"Just a moment. I'll be back shortly." Waiting only for her nod, he strode back the way they came, drips of water leading him along the path. He knew one of his bodyguards wouldn't be far off. Out of sight but within shouting distance. They were the instructions whenever he braved this area.

It didn't take long for them to accommodate his request, and he returned to Eva, heavy woollen blanket in hand. She hadn't shifted, the puddle at her feet creeping out farther still. She hadn't heard him walk back which gave him a moment to study her. Mascara was starting to run down her cheeks, and her once fashionable curls hung limp, pieces plastered to her face. The jacket hem hung in an odd fashion, completely sodden around the base, and most likely ruined, as would be her dress. He felt a pang for the loss of all her hard work, ruined by one stupid act.

He expected her to be distressed, but other than looking cold she appeared quite at peace. The shuffle of his shoe hitting a pebble had her head snapping back toward him, away from the roses she'd been studying.

He held up the blanket, closing the distance between them. Settling it about her shoulders. He discarded the idea of requesting she shed his wet jacket and dress first so she wasn't huddled in sodden clothing. A man could only take so much.

"Thanks." Her voice was breathless, and he knew she was as affected by him as he was by her.

He searched for something to say, anything to stop himself from diving into those delicious lips that called to him.

"Do you know what type of roses they are?"

It wasn't quite the bucket of water he needed but it would do. Dropping his hands from the blanket, he pocketed them, and turned his gaze to the section of the maze they'd reached. Some of the blooms held a mauve tinge, their fragrance overpowering his senses. Last time he'd been here he'd felt so twisted on the inside he thought something would break. He could still recall the sweat that had broken out everywhere, like every pore was physically rejecting his being there. Part of him still tingled with the memories. A tiny voice urged him to leave, but a louder voice wouldn't let him give up this time with Eva.

Being in here, with her, was in some way healing. The sense of being all alone and trapped wasn't so prevalent. She was somehow shining a light on the darkness he struggled with.

"Queen Aristotle. I think. I could have Stefan check for you if you like. Do you like roses?"

"Does any woman not like roses?"

He let the grin spread across his face at her answer. He shrugged off the sense that he was stepping through the walls he'd built for himself. Eva had been through a shocking day, what would it hurt to be there for her?

"Are they your favourite flower?" He knew as he spoke the words that they weren't. She loved Lily of the Valley. Or at least she had, once upon a time.

"No. My favourite's the same." She looked at him then, searching his eyes, clearly finding the answer she was looking for. "So, do you still drink coffee like it's going out of fashion?"

"We don't do it as well here as the Italians, but yes. I managed to encourage a friend of mine who owns a café in town to use imported beans. He complains about the cost but never about the line out of the door during the mornings. It's not the same though, when I drink coffee here. I've decided part of the appeal of coffee in Italy is the ambience."

"How do you mean?"

"Everyone is so relaxed along that strip of coastline. They fish, they walk, they sit and enjoy life. I was able to adopt that whilst there ..."

He let the words drift. For once, the silence between them wasn't charged with unanswered questions. They'd reached a truce, falling into the pattern from when they'd first met. It was comforting to know they hadn't lost that connection. He was thankful she didn't press him for answers he didn't know how to explain.

———

Eva's mind was awash with memories. She itched to reach out and take Henrik's hand, feel the burn of their fingers coming into contact, shooting fire and life into her veins. It hadn't gone away, five years and countless other hands had been shaken, but none had given her the same connection.

She didn't dare give in to the idea, nor speak any of the questions that were hammering in her head. For once they were alone and she just wanted to enjoy that feeling. It was the first time she'd felt calm since arriving in his country. Not that the experience had been filled with anything but luxury, but she'd been on edge, feeling like an imposter.

Walking with him right now, she didn't feel that. She just felt like the Eva he'd met in Italy. The one who'd fallen headlong in love with him, much to the detriment of her heart.

"Are roses your mum's favourite flower?"

His mouth thinned, one end dipping in sadness. It was like the sun had slid behind a cloud. She sensed it hurt him to be here, her question just now confirming that fact.

"She did love roses, yes. But wisteria was her favourite."

Was? He spoke past tense, creating a chasm of sorrow within her. What had happened to his mother? She pushed the shadowy thought aside, vowing to shift their conversation onto another topic. She didn't want to risk any sort of subject that would lead to their bubble breaking.

"Wisteria and a matching lilac gate. It's exquisitely beautiful and calming. Was there a reason for this being a maze?"

"Not particularly. My mother loved to garden, and after

she married my father, he had this land cleared so she could have a green space just for her. She designed this maze, complete with her own perfect oasis at the centre. Designing was in her blood. Like it is for you."

Eva smiled as heat bloomed in her cheeks, unsure how to respond. He'd remembered her love of design, did that mean he remembered all their time together? Did he still think of her?

"You haven't done anything with your designing? You're just working full time in tailoring?" His words were curious more than accusing, cutting into her own thoughts. *Probably for the best.*

"It's just not the right time to think about building up my own label. My grandfather's been sick—a bout of flu that he's been struggling to shake. Plus, he's developed the first stages of arthritis so long hours of stitching are almost out of the question now."

"Which puts the majority of the work on you?"

"Yes, but it's a big opportunity for me. You don't find a lot of women tailors, and he's given me the best training anyone could hope for. I get a lot of praise for my work. It's ... satisfying."

"Satisfying, but not where your true talent lies."

Eva shrugged. "I appreciate the praise," the words 'especially from you' floated in her mind, "but I'm being 100 percent honest when I say the timing is all wrong. Perhaps once Gramps' is back to full strength and can help me with fit sessions and customer service, I'll re-consider my options."

Henrik turned to her, grasping her hand which sent her heart spinning into an explosion of beats.

"You should. You're gifted Eva."

His words and focus made her strangely nervous. This

wasn't the carefree Henrik she'd met in Italy, he was a crown prince of a small European country. His responsibilities were endless, whilst hers were only to her gramps' and the business.

"The media coverage I'm currently getting is certainly encouraging. Felix seems to be working miracles."

She hated herself the moment she spoke Felix's name. Henrik's hand dropped from hers. She may as well have built a brick wall between them. But she needed the reminder of why she was here.

Felix was paying her to act as his girlfriend. A job she hadn't done well. Instead of keeping Harriet's claws off him, she'd stepped in front of the bus so to speak, then disappeared. She really shouldn't be indulging herself this time with Henrik. He wasn't the brother she was meant to be in love with. Not that she was still in love with him—that

would be crazy. Their time in Italy was just what he called it, a fantasy. Nothing that resembled reality. She knew she still had feelings invested though, and she needed to take care, or she'd find herself falling back into treasured memories far too easily.

Henrik kept walking for a few steps before he spun on his heel and returned to stand right before her.

"Promise me you won't give up your passion." He hooked a lock of wet hair behind her ear. It tickled as a droplet ran down the side of her neck, tingling with awareness. Heat spread from the small contact of his finger lingering a second too long.

When he looked at her like that, she wanted to promise him anything.

9

———

enrik paced about the library. The ice in the glass clinked as he brought the amber liquid to his lips. Its fiery burn did nothing to soothe him. His trip to Brussels had been annoying and could easily have been handled by Felix. Except his brother appeared to be too busy with Eva to take on any further royal engagements.

Jealousy engulfed him, but he shoved it aside.

At least Eva seemed to be coping with the media and being in the spotlight. That surprised him, though it shouldn't have. The time they'd spent together in Italy, she'd had an innate sense of calm, of inner strength.

She'd looked so natural in front of the press, her voice level, no fidgeting in sight.

All photos of Eva soaking wet at the garden party were disposed of, a task he'd seen to personally. Not that she didn't look beautiful, and very appealing, in all the photos he'd purchased, but he knew she wouldn't want that kind of press. It was something he could do, one small thing that eased his mind.

He longed to kiss her again. Their time in the rose

garden showed him their connection was every bit as strong now as it had been before. But it was no use, even seeing her coping as she was. Love held no place in the life he lived. He wouldn't allow it to be so, opening himself up to that ... no. It was better this way.

Taking another mouthful of scotch, he hardened the wall around his heart. It would be better for everyone this way.

The soft knock at the door had him turning from the window. Sophia offered a smile as she moved into the room and headed for the drinks cabinet.

"What's your poison?"

"Glenfiddich."

"Eww. That is poison. Is there brandy in here?"

"Let me get it for you."

She waved him off, instead lifting and sniffing at the contents until she found what suited her. Henrik allowed his mouth to lift in a small smile. Most people assumed Lady Sophia to be quiet and demure. Those who knew her better made no such mistake.

"So, state dinner. Should be fun." Sophia's words were teasing.

Henrik sighed, knowing it would be anything but.

"Yes, tonnes of fun. Did I ever thank you for agreeing to bring forward your visit? I know you had other plans."

"Yes, you've already thanked me. A few times." She drew her eyebrows together in thought. "I love visiting here—you know that. Izzie is such fun and Eva is an absolute delight. I only hope she doesn't get hurt."

Henrik nodded in agreement, the bitter taste on his tongue nothing to do with his drink. Throwing back the remaining liquid, he moved to stand next to Sophia, refilling his own glass to halfway. Ignoring Sophia's raised brow, he took a seat beside the fire, the heat blasting one side of his body.

"Izzie said things between you and Felix are still off. That it almost seems to be worse since you got back from London ... Did something happen there?"

Other than Felix toying with the only woman he'd ever loved? "No."

"I can see you're in a talkative mood." Sophia's smile was mocking.

Sighing, Henrik took a large swallow, taking his time replying. "I don't know what's happened with Felix and I, but it's been going on longer than London. You know that."

"I do. I guess I just wondered if it had something to do with Eva."

"Why would you think that?" Henrik's words came out sharper than he meant them too. He inwardly winced when Sophia narrowed her gaze at him.

"Because of that there." She pointed to his eyes. "You get this look about you whenever her name is mentioned. Last night when you were speaking about her it almost seemed like ... I couldn't put my finger on it but you're doing it again. You're trying to hide something."

Henrik stood and moved away from Sophia's prying eyes.

"Henrik, how long have we known each other?"

"Too long, I think."

Sophia chuckled. "Gee thanks. Look, I think we've known each other and been friends long enough that we can be totally honest with each other, without judgement. If we're going to be married, honesty is going to be one of the main things that will keep us sane."

Sophia was right. She deserved his total honesty.

"You make a good point." Turning, Henrik looked at his

friend. "I have met Eva before. I met her five years ago when I was in Italy."

"Five years ago? Wait, I remember you telling me about that trip. Is she the one? Is Eva the woman you fell in love with?"

"Yes."

"Wow! Talk about a bombshell. So, what happened?"

"It doesn't matter. It wouldn't have worked."

"Seriously? That's all I get? Why wouldn't it have worked? Didn't she love you back?"

"It just wouldn't have worked out."

"Henrik, I say this with love and as your friend, possibly your only friend: you're being a total git. Does Felix know? That you and Eva have a past?"

"I haven't mentioned it to him. I don't know if Eva has." He hesitated on adding more.

"You hesitated. What aren't you telling me?"

"I kind of pretended I didn't know her. When I saw her again. In London." The look on Sophia's face was comical.

"Henrik that's just outright rude! What's the matter with you?"

"It gets worse. I left out ..." he circled a finger around his head, "... the crown factor, when I first met her in Italy."

Stunned silence met his words.

Recovering quickly, Sophia polished off her own drink before continuing. "Let me get this straight. You met Eva in Italy, lied about being a crown prince, fell in love but then walked away from her for no good reason, and now she's met Felix and is dating him? And he's brought her here to the palace for a visit?"

"Well, officially she's here as a tailor, though Izzie has highjacked her to design a ballgown for the Winter Ball."

"But she and Felix *are* dating."

"Appearances would suggest so." He still didn't want to believe it, but he didn't care to share those insights with Sophia.

"Do you still love her?"

Five words. One question. One that he refused to answer.

He took his time before settling on a casual shrug, downing the rest of his drink. Again. "It doesn't matter."

Henrik moved towards the drinks cabinet, his path stilled by the hand laid gently on his arm. Sophia turned him to look at her fully. "It matters if you still love her, Henrik. Felix has only just met her; how are you going to live with that if he falls for her?"

Her words punched him in the gut. Just hearing Eva's name next to Felix's made his blood boil. He knew oh too well how easily one could fall for Eva. Did he really think Felix would be immune? Curling his long fingers into fists, he resisted the urge to punch the wall. He'd set aside his desires to go find Eva for years. Having her right in the palace was torture, but he didn't have any other choice.

"Sophia, I appreciate you looking out for me, I do. But I don't have anything to offer Eva. You and I both know the kind of life and pressures expected of someone married to me and my title. I thought we agreed on that?"

"I agree your wife will constantly be in the spotlight, will be followed by media and scrutinised by the citizens of Stenaco. I agreed to say yes if you offer that role to me, because it also helps me out and I'm not interested in love. But Henrik, if you have been lucky enough to find someone who you love, you can't walk away from that. I don't under-stand why you would want to?"

"Love wouldn't be enough to save Eva from being my wife."

"Save her? Honestly, Henrik, you're not making sense."

"Then let's leave it. Please. I've made my decision."

Refilling his glass, Henrik could feel the first tendrils of an alcoholic haze seeping into his brain. It didn't stop him taking another fortifying gulp. Dinner would be an ordeal, made worse now that he'd told Sophia about his past with Eva.

She brushed past him, shaking her head and muttering about him being a stubborn fool. She waited at the door, presumably for him to escort her to dinner, her arms folded, and brows scrunched together in thought.

Henrik didn't disagree with Sophia, but love hadn't been enough to save his mother.

He couldn't risk seeing the same thing happen to Eva.

Eva was nervous. She thanked her every fashion instinct that she'd chosen black for her dress which would hide any possible sweat marks. The dress was simple yet elegant, something she'd been able to put together quickly in the few days since the disastrous garden party, and in between working on Izzie's gown. She'd wanted to hide but Felix had insisted it would be better for her to be seen out and about. She'd scoured the papers for images of her imitating a drowned rat but so far hadn't found any.

When Felix had mentioned a state dinner Eva had agreed, hoping it wouldn't be too bad. Then he'd turned up at her room, in full royal dress, and all Eva could think of was seeing Henrik. Would he be similarly attired? Felix had insisted she wear a ruby-encrusted necklace, with matching filigree earrings and a dainty tiara. She couldn't begin to imagine what they cost. The long walk across the palace to the formal dining room hadn't been enough to recover her shredded nerves.

"Eva, you might want to breathe. You're turning blue."

Felix's words penetrated her panicked thoughts and she realised he was right. Breathing would help. In fact, it was rather essential to not keeling over on the spot, which would draw attention to her. Right now, that would be too much to handle.

"Right. Sorry. I thought you said it was a small state dinner?"

His soft laugh floated at her ear. "Did I? Relax, you look beautiful."

Eva wanted to roll her eyes. Clearly, Felix thought she was worried about her appearance. Her eyes tracked around the room, falling on her real reason for worry. Try as she had, she wasn't prepared for seeing Henrik decked out in his royal uniform.

She wanted to smack herself in the face but had to settle for a stern mental talking to. When would she stop thinking about him? She'd spent most of the day with Sophia, whose warm praise and sincere interest was proof that Sophia was as close to perfect as a person could come. Henrik deserved someone perfect. She'd accepted that. Why should the change in attire or type of dinner even matter?

Who was she kidding? It didn't matter. She'd have been this nervous regardless. All the mental pep talking in the world couldn't stop her treacherous heart from dancing at the sight of him. Her blood ran green when he placed a hand at Sophia's waist. Could she be a more horrible person? Sophia had gone out of her way to help her today with business suggestions and industry contacts, and here she was, drooling over Sophia's future husband.

Felix cleared his throat in a pointed fashion. "Eva? Have you been listening?"

"Um, sorry, no. Distracted by all the gorgeous dresses. You know me. Can't help myself." Hoping Felix wouldn't notice the high pitch to her voice, she spotted a waiter closing in on them, holding a tray of liquid courage. Smiling in thanks, she took a large gulp of champagne. The chilled bubbles threatening to burst out her nose at her exuberance. She wasn't much of a drinker, more prone to cups of tea than flutes of Moët. Her eyes watered slightly as she wrinkled her nose, dispersing the feeling.

"Maybe try for a sip next time." Amusement laced Felix's words.

"Yep. Sorry about that."

Her contrite expression garnered a full-blown laugh from the man beside her. Enough to have Henrik's gaze flashing in their direction. For a moment, his eyes locked with hers. His deepened, almost appearing black. The touch of Felix's hand on the small of her back broke the connection.

"Let me introduce you to my father."

"Hmm? What! Wait, the king?" Her squeak was back, not that Felix noticed as he moved her to the windows where a group of men stood. Her nerves came back in force. Why did Felix want to introduce her to his father? How would meeting his father help Felix? Did their charade really need to go that far?

"Father, this is Eva James."

The man who turned in their direction was an older version of Henrik. His jet-black hair was laced with grey, and his azure gaze took in everything at a glance. Slight creases wrinkled at the edge of his eyes. He was wider through the middle but still looked in good shape. His face broke into a smile which had memories of a similar smile in Italy flashing in her mind.

"My son speaks highly of you, Miss James. Welcome to our country. I trust you're enjoying your stay so far?"

Eva started nodding before realising that she was standing before royalty, executing a quick curtsy she hoped was passable.

"Yes, Your Highness. Your country is spectacular. Thank you for allowing me to stay here." She cringed inwardly at her gushing words. Could she sound more simple?

His gaze shifted to her left just as she felt a new presence there. Her body instinctively knew who stood beside her.

"Henrik, perhaps you could see to Miss James for a moment. I need to speak to Felix."

Equal parts joy and despair shot through Eva as she watched Felix walk away with his father. Why did Henrik keep showing up just as Felix needed to go elsewhere?

"You don't need to babysit me. I'm a big girl; I can mingle."

"How are you enjoying your time in Stenaco so far? I hope Izzie isn't creating too much work for you?"

Okay. Seemed he was going to ignore her offer of an out. Part of her was elated by his choice. That part was dancing and singing old-school love songs which featured Henrik as he was currently dressed, sweeping her off her feet. She ignored that part.

"Izzie's only requested the one outfit. Someone very kindly sent me a seamstress and she's been a godsend with helping me find local suppliers and arranging fabrics to be shipped in from Paris. I think Izzie will love it."

Eva resolutely kept her gaze out over the crowd, admiring the sea of glittered dresses and enough jewellery to hurt the eyes.

"I'm glad Mabel has been helpful. Lorenzo recommended her as the best for your needs. May I see it sometime? The dress?"

She swung towards him, nearly spilling her glass of champagne.

"You sent Mabel?" Shock must have been written all over her face, but she couldn't disguise her feelings. Henrik was the last person she'd been expecting help from.

Her only answer was a slight movement of his left shoulder. Had he sent her in guilt? Was this another form of apology? His expression gave nothing away, barricaded behind a mask. She was beginning to realise this was the expression he always adopted when carrying out royal activities.

"Thank you." She continued to look at him as she spoke the words. Memorising his features, this Henrik whose world she didn't know at all and didn't belong in, but who still showed pockets of the old Henrik she'd loved. She struggled to connect the two, unsure which was the real deal.

An orchestra struck up, music drifting out amongst the guests. Groups that had been scattered about the ballroom drifted to the edges to continue their conversations, whilst others coupled to dance. Eva craned her neck to see if she could spy Felix, sure that Henrik would need to excuse himself to dance with Sophia.

Henrik stepped into her line of vision, one hand offered towards her, the other crooked behind his back. It was all so formal, as if she'd stumbled into a fairy tale by accident. She braced for contact as she accepted his hand. She could feel the rough patches on her fingers, so different to the softness of his palm. Her hand was cold, the warmth in his instantly sending waves of heat up her arms and to other areas. She didn't stop to give Felix or

Sophia one more thought as she was pulled into Henrik's strong embrace.

Time slipped away as he waltzed her around the room. She'd learnt to dance with her Gramps, his love of old films rubbing off on Eva as she'd grown up. She was thankful for that now, though Henrik already knew she could waltz, had remembered.

This was a dream come true. Eva felt so safe in Henrik's arms, so at home—even though she was in a situation that was beyond her wildest thoughts—because he was holding her, that all drifted away. Her time in his country so far had been a whirlwind of events, each and every one glamorous but not once had she felt calm, and like herself. Right now, being held by Henrik, she felt more herself than ever before. Her mind tried to butt in—to tell her this wasn't real, but she refused to let it, marvelling only in this one moment.

She breathed deep, picking out the starch on his uniform mingling with his own unique smell. A heavy after-shave, seductive hints of citrus and refreshing spice with an undercurrent of leather that had haunted her for years. She remembered an afternoon in Harrods, going through the male scents department, wasting close to an hour trying to find a memory of him. She hadn't found what she'd been searching for; he'd been as elusive then as he was now.

That thought had her jerking back from him slightly. It would cause a scene to walk away from him mid-dance, but she was getting too close, her memories causing her to forget the current situation.

His eyes sought hers, a questioning glance within their depths. His arms loosened a little, like he'd read her mind. Had he sensed her unease?

"You never answered my question before. About the dress?"

Racking her brain, Eva tried to bring to mind what he'd asked. Izzie's dress. That was right—he'd wanted to see it.

"Why? I mean, sorry, yes, you may see it, of course. But why do you want to?"

He studied her for a moment, like he was searching for an answer in her gaze. She was bewildered by his actions at present, like he was struggling between the version of Henrik she'd met in Italy and the real Henrik. She cleared her throat slightly, deciding she didn't want to wait for his answer, unsure as to whether he was even going to give her one. "You should probably be dancing with your *fiancée.*"

The word stuck slightly on her tongue. Here she was, dressed in a beautiful ballgown, complete with borrowed crown jewels, dancing with the man of her dreams. But none of it was real.

Henrik struggled to keep up with the emotions flashing across Eva's exquisite face. He wanted to refute her comment, that Sophia wasn't his fiancée, but remained mute. He'd been unable to stop his feet from walking towards her when she'd entered the room, especially seeing Felix taking her over to their father. He'd wanted to be the one to introduce her, be at her side, but had no reason to do so. Inviting her to dance with him? Stupidity. Why was he torturing himself this way?

He should answer her. It served him better if she thought he was engaged. He had made up his mind, hadn't he? He'd marry Sophia, take the safe option. His heart held other ideas, but he couldn't listen to it.

"I managed to bury any photos of your visit into the

pond." Why had he said that? He hadn't been going to tell Eva. His three glasses of scotch were taking their toll.

"Oh! Thank you ... I was wondering why I hadn't seen anything." A brief shadow crossed her features.

It was heaven holding her in his arms again. He was man enough to admit he'd imagined what it would feel like, having her at a state event, the envy of all other men in the room. She looked stunning. There was no other word for it. Her solid black gown hugged her slight curves, showcasing her long legs whenever she took a step. It was refined, unlike a lot of the other over-dressed women in the room.

Eva's high heels brought the top of her head almost level with his nose. Which placed the tiara she was wearing directly in his line of sight. It was delicate, one of the much lesser from the royal collection, but it had been one of his mother's favourites. He expected to feel a twinge at seeing it but was surprised it didn't come. Instead, there was only a sense of warmth. Eva looked so serene and calm, like she wore tiaras and danced at state dinners every other day.

Her brows were still knitted together.

"Is something the matter?"

"Why did you kill the story of my falling into the pond?" She blurted the words, her lashes sheltering her eyes, preventing him from attempting to read her emotions.

"I felt responsible for Harriet's actions. I should have realised earlier she was out to create problems for you and done something to prevent any further retaliation."

"Surely it should be Felix who would see to that ... I am here with him."

Five little words that were like a kick in the groin. Why did he keep forgetting that so easily?

He chose not to comment further, instead finishing the dance before walking her towards Izzie and Sophia. To others it would appear both women were simply enjoying the evening, but he'd known them long enough to recognise similar thoughtful looks. Just before they reached the others Henrik paused, his hand brushing against Eva's wrist to capture her attention.

"Eva ... even though things can't be different for us, I need you to know I wanted to come that night." He wanted to say more. He wanted to tell her he wished things could be different now. His mum's final warning kept his mouth shut. He needed to marry someone who could handle crown life.

10

*E*va toyed with the silver beaded bracelet at her wrist. Last night had been ... odd. In some ways it had been everything she'd been dreaming of. Being held in Henrik's arms ... that one dance would feed her heart for years. His parting words were bittersweet but somehow they'd thawed the last of the frustration she felt towards him. He had been a crown prince then, just as much as he was now—it didn't really matter why he hadn't been able to turn up. She was never going to be royal material, so she needed to just move on. She'd glimpsed bits of the softer Henrik. He'd smiled and even laughed at Izzie's antics. Knowing that the man she'd met in Italy was still in there somewhere, settled her mind.

Felix hadn't reappeared, not even for dinner, which had left her feeling a bit like she needn't be there. But Sophia, Izzie and Henrik had stuck close all evening. She'd surprised herself by how relaxed she'd felt in their company, dressed as she was. The dinner that had followed had been delicious, though seeing Sophia and Henrik seated together had brought her back to earth from the bubble she'd floated off into for a while. He'd only danced with her to fill the time, probably as an apology for his brother not returning. Pity dancing.

Enough! Wallowing didn't suit her, and honestly it wasn't at all helpful to her real reason for being at the palace. As far as she could tell she was holding up her end of the bargain. She hadn't seen Harriet again since the garden party, and Felix had said she was acting like a great cover. Of course, that would be easier if he was actually around. She didn't like to feel like she was taking advantage of this deal, and even though she'd done a little tailoring for Felix it didn't appear as if he was getting as much out of this agreement as she was. Guess it was too late to change much now. She barely had ten days left until she'd leave—walk away from Stenaco and from Henrik forever.

Rolling her eyes at her thoughts, always so happy to stray back to Henrik, she pulled out this morning's paper that had been delivered to her room amongst a whole stack. The Stenish papers had mainly focused on a new regime being passed by parliament but a few of the London papers had run articles on her and Felix. It amazed her how quickly the media had turned them into a great love story. They'd been out a few times, yes, but mainly in groups with other people. The only real show of 'relationship' was that one surprise kiss outside the nightclub.

She was starting to learn though that the media could be quite creative when it came to reporting news. Her face was plastered on the front of the *Star*. Not a paper she ever read whilst home, but since it mentioned her, she'd plucked it out of the pile. It wasn't a flattering article. Portraying her as a wanna-be designer with only mild talent, snide comments about her trying too hard, and wearing a style that apparently washed her out. Part of her wanted to just laugh it away, but a bigger part was seriously hurt. She'd felt really good last night, and now this article was tainting that feeling.

It was hard to say if the article was really about her or Felix, given there were an array of other women featured in the article too. It showcased his penchant for socialites and actresses, with her being the strange exception. Part of the article even hinted she was using him simply to gain a social following, to increase her popularity.

Deliberately folding the paper in half, trapping the offending article inside, she tossed it into the bin. The thud was satisfying, and whilst it wasn't so easy to eradicate the feelings the article evoked, it was at least lying where it belonged.

A soft knock at the door had Eva lifting her gaze. She was expecting Felix, so was surprised to see Henrik stride through. He was in a suit, its fit beautiful, leaving Eva impressed by its maker. She'd briefly met Henrik's tailor, an older Italian gentleman who was friendly and had spoken highly of her gramps—a fact which added to her immediate respect for the man.

Lorenzo knew how to promote power through the subtle lines of his work. Not that Henrik needed much help— sovereignty radiated from his every pore. Something in the way he stood, always holding himself just so, made her think of movies where knights stood ready to battle, fight for their kingdoms ... fight for the beautiful princesses sitting in their towers.

There went her fanciful thoughts again. She stood, offering an awkward bow, which thankfully went unnoticed as Henrik's gaze was caught by something over at the side of her workroom.

"That's impressive work, Eva. Has Izzie seen it?"

Eva moved from behind her desk to stand next to Henrik at the mannequin. The dress was a way from being finished, part of it held together with pins. The skirt layers were mostly done; the layer closest to the skin had only arrived from the Parisian embroidery house yesterday. She planned to add some more detail to it herself, hoping to ensure the flowers really popped as they were glimpsed through the wearer's legs. The bodice still needed some internal structure, but the silk organza pleating was looking dreamy and romantic, just as she'd planned.

"Izzie came for a fitting yesterday. Hopefully it'll work, and as she moves it will appear as if she's walking through a field of flowers, the skirts billowing behind her. That's the idea anyway." Warmth rose in her cheeks as she spoke the words.

"It's beautiful."

Eva glanced at Henrik only to find him studying her. Swallowing to remove the dryness that had taken over her mouth, she slid her eyes back to the dress. Lifting the top layer, she fiddled with the embroidery, its shiny surface smooth against her fingers. She puffed the layer out a little, watching it drift back into place. Coughing to hide her pleasure at his praise, she walked back over to her desk to sit down.

"Have you seen your brother? He never returned to the dinner last night."

"Actually, that's why I'm here. Felix had to go away on some urgent state business; he won't be back in the capital for a week. He left last night."

Her mouth formed an *O*, but no sound emitted. *Nice of Felix to come tell her himself.*

"I'm sorry Felix couldn't tell you himself. He did leave me this to give you though."

Removing a sealed envelope from his breast pocket, he handed it to her. Their fingers touched briefly before she snatched hers away. Opening the seal with fingers that trembled, she removed the thick parchment with a few scrawled words.

Apologies, Eva. Father has commanded me away. At least this makes our cover nice and easy. Don't fret; this won't change our deal. Yours, F

Huffing a short breath, Eva took care to re-fold the paper and return it to its home.

Henrik heard Eva's small sigh. She was disappointed. Bitterness rang through him, making him wonder again at what was written in the letter. He'd struggled with an intense desire to break his brother's trust, to read his words. In the end, common sense had won.

"Thanks for bringing it to me. At least now I won't have any distractions from finishing your sister's gown."

Her smile didn't reach her eyes and Henrik ached to reach out and take her in his arms. "I hope Izzie hasn't been causing you grief over her dress. She can be a bit demanding at times."

"Not at all; it's a dream opportunity for me. Your sister is lovely."

He let out a short laugh; he couldn't help it. Lovely was not a word one normally used with Izzie. Cheeky, feisty, most definitely loveable ... but not lovely. "Don't let Izzie hear you calling her lovely. She'll be pissed off."

"Why is that?" Eva's smile shone across her whole face, her head tipped to the side with her question. Henrik had been standing before her desk but moved to prop himself against the corner, looking down at her. Her hair was scraped up into a clip and had probably been neat at one stage today.

The scrunched pieces of paper about the desk told him she'd been agonising over her work. He'd seen her like this in Italy, after one of their passionate interludes. He'd found her sketching furiously by moonlight, out on the small deck of her hotel room. She'd been so engrossed in what she was drawing she hadn't heard him. He'd been transfixed by her passion, her beauty. The following day he'd snuck a look at her sketches, marvelling at her talent.

The memory faded along with Eva's smile. Her lips parted, revealing the soft pink of her tongue as it flicked across her bottom lip. Her eyes fled from his to focus on the letter she still held. He thought he detected a gleam of desire before they broke contact.

Reaching out, he spun her chair to face him, his other hand plucking the letter from her fingers and tossing it on the table.

"Eva." His voice was a soft command.

Trailing a finger across her cheek, he hooked a rogue strand of chocolate hair behind her ear. Its silky texture taunted him as he let his finger continue its path down the side of her throat. Her pulse jumped in tune with his own heartbeat.

Leaning down, he placed his hands next to hers on the arm of the chair, trapping her with his body. He wanted to taste her, devour her where she sat. Common sense evaporated as he placed butterfly kisses along the path his finger had just taken. Her head fell back, eyes shuttering closed as she gave him greater access to the soft, sweet column of her neck.

"Open your eyes."

Thick lashes fluttered open to reveal her eyes, dreamy and laden with desire. Specks of light made them appear almost caramel in colour. Eyes he'd drowned in before.

"Say my name." He wanted to hear his name on her lips. Needed to hear it.

"Henrik." It was barely perceptible, whispered on a laboured breath. But it was all the invitation he needed. Lowering his head, he captured her mouth, savouring each delicious taste. Her tongue shot out to meet his, but he gently pushed back, keeping the pace slow. Shifting his hands, he captured her fingers, entwining them with his own.

Pulling back slightly, he let his forehead fall against hers. He didn't know why he was torturing himself. This time when her eyes opened, they drilled straight into his heart. The small taste wasn't enough. Time stopped as the only sound he could hear was her soft breathing. Cursing himself he dived right back in, this time letting all his pent-up passion loose.

Gone was the subtle exploration, replaced by blazing need. He sucked on her bottom lip. Memories of what she liked from their previous lovemaking had him rewarded by her husky groan. Placing his knee between her thighs he could feel her intimate heat, the sensation eliciting his own sounds of pleasure. The move tightened his already restricted pants. Capturing her face in his hands, he angled to deepen the kiss. She met his kisses, each more driven than the last. Kissing her with urgency, he demanded her surrender.

Taking one last taste he broke away, hanging his head next to hers. Heat emanated between them, his body aching to return to the blissful pleasure of her lips. He drew on years of practice, shutting down his emotions.

Pushing off the chair, he walked to the windows, unable to leave the room in his current state. "I'm sorry. I need to stop kissing you."

She didn't answer. The slam of the connecting door to her guest suite made him wince. He was acting like the wanker she'd called him last week. Why couldn't he keep his resolve when he was around her?

Because he still had feelings for her—that was why. Deep feelings that he'd hidden from these past years.

He allowed his head to slump against the windowsill. His mother's last words floated in his mind, reminding him he had no place living a life of passion and love, yet this time they weren't as helpful to his decision.

11

Eva spent the remainder of the day holed up in her bedroom. She couldn't charge Henrik entirely; she was as much to blame for the kiss as he was. Their connection was still there, of that she was sure, but it wasn't enough. Oh, and there was the small fact she was supposedly dating his brother, not to mention the added complication of his fiancée, the beautiful Lady Sophia.

By seven o'clock, hunger pains forced her to rally into leaving her self-imposed exile. Deciding to search out the kitchens, she opened her door and nearly collided with a blond wiry man she'd seen glued to Henrik's side the night before.

"Oh! Sorry."

Her words turned to a frown as she noticed he held a tray laden with silver cloches over dinner plates.

"Miss James, his Highness noticed you didn't appear for dinner so requested I bring you this."

"Right. Um. Thanks." Realising she was staring like a stuffed chicken, she moved from her spot blocking the doorway. Wringing her hands, she followed as he placed the tray on the small table that sat alongside the windows. "Is this normal protocol?"

For the first time, he smiled. "No, not really."

"I see. Can you please thank him for me?" She cringed inwardly at her words, transported back to school years with peers passing around notes in class. Could she sound more ... lame?

"Consider me thanked."

Henrik's velvety voice had her spinning back towards her door. She should have known he wouldn't let her hide away forever. She watched as Stefan offered a brief bow to Henrik then left the room. The click of the door felt ominous.

Eva crossed her arms and waited. Her stomach protested, loudly, at the proximity of food. Delicious smells wafted her way, but she refused to budge.

"Please eat, Eva."

"I'll wait until you go, if it's all the same to you."

The corner of his mouth quirked, showing signs of an actual smile. "I guess I deserve that. Would it help if I apologised for earlier?"

"That would depend on if you're apologising because you feel badly about your behaviour or if you're just trying to appease me."

His pause was long before he allowed his full smile to come through. Ignoring her words, he marched her over to the table and pulled the seat out as an obvious command to sit. Eva considered refusing, but only until he removed the cloche, revealing a plate of vibrant green basil linguine. Steam tendrils floated towards her, enticing her legs to bend of their own will. Damn him, he'd remembered.

Taking the seat opposite, he poured two glasses of wine. The glass chilled immediately, its contents tempting. The whole meal was a walk down memory lane, putting her on edge. She managed a few mouthfuls of the delicious meal whilst they sat in silence, Henrik watching her like a hawk. What was he playing at?

"I've come to offer a truce." His words were measured, his face returned to an unreadable mask. She took a sip of wine. "I'd like us to be friends."

Heat blossomed in her cheeks as the need to draw in air was hindered by the liquid caught in her thought. She knew it wasn't her best look. After a small round of embarrassing coughs, she offered a disbelieving response. "Why?"

"We were friends once before, Eva."

"No, we weren't. I don't know what label to put on that time, but we weren't 'friends'! Friends don't lie to each other, Your Highness." Sarcasm crept into her voice. She knew it didn't become her, but it helped shield her true feelings. Helped to guard the hope dying in her chest.

"Please, Eva. I'd like to show you around, make sure you enjoy the last few days of your time here."

Her eyes had been glued to the delectable meal before her but now, she flicked them to his. He wanted to spend time with her? Why?

Sighing, he seemed to read the unasked question on her face. "I understand your reluctance, but I assure you there will be no repeat of today's kiss. I've cleared my schedule tomorrow morning. I'll see you at nine."

Henrik stood, pushing his chair in, clearly accepting her silence as capitulation to his plans.

"Wait! What if I don't want to?"

"Then do it for Felix. It was his request." Henrik's long strides quickly covered the space between the table and the door.

Henrik's parting words killed the last vestiges of her

hunger. She'd wanted space from Henrik to think but now he'd left she felt bereft. Somehow, she'd hoped his offer to spend time with her was an olive branch. A part of her still loved Henrik, a big part, if she was being totally honest, and she wanted to get to know the royal version of him. As much as she didn't want it to, it hurt that he was only offering to spend time with her because of a request by Felix.

Sometime around midnight, Henrik gave up all pretence of sleep. After leaving Eva, he'd attempted to do some work but to no avail. A gruelling workout had left him physically exhausted but mentally, his thoughts still swirled around the kiss. He was unable to forget the taste of her on his lips. Just the thought of it had him semi-aroused.

Why was he torturing himself by spending time with her? He had been misjudging his ability to remain immune to her since she arrived. The club ... the fitting ... he could still remember the frustration that had been, standing there half-naked as she twirled her tape measure about. He kept ordering himself to remain strong but kept slipping.

He walked to his window, cracking it open. He welcomed the icy tendrils of wind as they wrapped around his naked body.

Their connection had been immediate, when she'd first stumbled into his arms in Italy. He hadn't been looking for anything on that trip apart from his freedom. It had been his mother's suggestion to 'take a week off'. His father hadn't been thrilled but had grudgingly allowed it. Ten days, he'd been a nobody, just an average university student, back-packing around Italy over the summer holidays. The press had been fed lies about him being abroad in Australia; it was the one and only time he'd managed to really feel unshackled from the crown. He couldn't shake the thought that it had been a farewell gift from his mum.

Would Eva have felt the same connection if he'd been upfront with her from the start? All his life, the girls he'd dated had been vetted, had pedigrees, had connections. He wasn't a saint, but he made sure he was discreet and there were no false hopes. He'd never lied to a woman—except Eva. He still struggled to forgive himself for the deception.

He'd planned to tell her the truth when they'd agreed to meet at the little cafe in Monterosso. He had practiced his words of love in the mirror, nervous as to how she would react. Surely her feelings for him would help her forgive his ruse. She hadn't yet voiced her feelings but when their eyes met, he had no doubt her love mirrored his own.

Then the phone call from his father—his mother ... Even now he couldn't complete the memory in his mind. He'd agonised over leaving without going to see Eva. To tell her he'd get in touch when he could. Devastated at the news of his mother, he had decided to wait.

He had Eva's full contact details—not one of his proudest moments, but after their first meeting, he'd needed to know who she was. He had her address; he would track her down and explain.

Except explanations hadn't come. The missed phone message he'd found from two days prior, shattered his world. Had he not been so wrapped up in his own bid for freedom, he would have taken the call. Perhaps he could have saved his mum. Why had he been such a fool, not listening to the voicemail until it was too late?

It was in the past now, even if his heart still ached for a way to change it all. He'd made a promise to Sophia and he would keep it. His heart may still long for Eva, but it wasn't to be. She was a dream he couldn't have, a memory that had to stay just that.

He could offer her friendship though. To ensure she enjoyed his country as much as possible. He would be selfish, let him be his true self tomorrow, before he walked away for good. He would give her a full explanation of the events surrounding his mother, then ensure he stayed away from her until she left Stenaco.

12

"So, where to first?" Eva pasted a smile on her face, hoping it would detract from the dark rings under her eyes. She'd given up on sleep in the early hours of the morning. Images of her and Henrik together had plagued her dreams, leaving her wanting and breathless when she'd woken. Feeling bereft that it was only a dream, she'd decided to grind out her frustrations on Izzie's gown. It was some of Eva's best work; she could only hope Izzie would love it as much as she did.

"I thought we'd take a drive. There are markets down by the water." Henrik stepped up to the black SUV, opening the door for Eva to get in.

She'd dressed casually, unsure about their plans. The thought of spending the whole morning with Henrik, along with her lack of sleep, had put her on edge. The classic navy slacks teamed with a soft wool jumper and leather flats were on the boring side. She'd attempted to put some colour into the ensemble with a printed silk scarf, edged with tiny pom-poms which hopped about as she walked. Henrik was similarly attired in casual clothing, so she allowed herself a small sigh of relief that she'd chosen correctly.

The procession of three SUV's moved down the long driveway, exited the palace gates with an array of flashing camera lights. It hadn't dawned on Eva until then that she would be seeing Henrik for the first time in public as royalty. Her nerves tripled at the thought of being on show.

"Is there anything in particular you'd like to see?" Henrik's dry words cut into her thoughts.

"Um. No." Well done, Eva, conversational genius.

"Would you prefer we don't chat?" Henrik turned in his seat to face her, his eyes boring into her own. She shifted uncomfortably at the assessment.

"I guess I'm just nervous. I'm used to being in the background. I like the background. You don't really do 'background'."

"No. My position doesn't allow me to be anything other than in the spotlight. My country loves its royal family, and I love my country. I would be doing them a disservice if I hid away."

The image of Henrik hiding in the bushes popped into her head. It was so ludicrous she let out a short bark of laughter.

Henrik lifted an eyebrow in question.

"Sorry, don't mind me. It was nothing."

"Your random outburst of laughter was nothing? C'mon, Eva. Don't leave me hanging." The smile that slid across Henrik's face was cheeky, his eyes glistening with interest.

"No, really. It was nothing. I just laugh randomly when I get nervous." 'Cause that sounded better? She wanted to slap herself in the face but resisted the urge.

"Okay. If you're going to be like that, I only have one solution."

Before she could register Henrik's intent, he leaned over into her personal space. Pinning her hands together he delivered a devilish tickling assault on her ribcage. Her high-pitched squeals bounced around along with their laughter. Eva had always been ticklish; it was one of the first things Henrik had uncovered about her during their time in Italy. It seemed he hadn't forgotten.

Struggling to breathe through her laughter and begging him to stop, she managed to twist one of her hands out to return the torture. The car jolted to a stop which had her falling into his lap. Their combined heavy breathing sounded conspicuously loud now that the car wasn't moving.

A deep clearing of a voice came from the front of the vehicle.

"Apologies, Your Highness, but we've arrived."

Heat blossomed over Eva's face as she briefly caught the eyes of the security guard in the rear-view mirror. She was plastered over Henrik's body and they were acting like five-year-olds on a long car trip. Lifting herself off his hard body, she focused on fixing her scarf and hair. Once she felt presentable again, she looked out the window, they were in some sort of underground car park. She hoped pictures of her lolling over Henrik wouldn't make news headline tomorrow.

"Thank you, Frank." Henrik's voice held a huskiness that had her eyes flicking back in his direction. He was looking directly at her, his face relaxed. Gone was the haughty impenetrable mask she'd come to expect; in its place was the Henrik she'd first met: open and inviting, his eyes dancing with hidden humour. He held his hand out for her to take, one eyebrow cocked in challenge.

Another memory popped into her mind, of them

constantly holding hands. It was a link neither had ever wanted to break. Ducking her head, she allowed herself a half smile. Warmth bloomed at the touch of his fingers when she slid hers into his grasp. Sliding out of the car beside him, her whole face broke out in amusement as he donned a baseball cap.

"What? It's my undercover prince look."

"Of course it is." Her voice matched his in huskiness, her hand squeezing his. She lifted her other hand to tuck a longer tuft of hair behind his ear. The heat that sprung in his eyes at her gesture had her back-pedalling. What was she doing? This wasn't a walk down Memory Lane. This was him agreeing to show her around because Felix had requested it. What was wrong with her?

Mentally and physically taking a step back, she locked her hands together in front of her, ensuring they didn't sneak off of their own accord again.

Henrik pointed to the exit, ushering her towards the path before shoving his hands into his jeans pockets. Cold air hit her once they reached the pavement, reminding her she should have brought her coat. Turning to ask to go back, she stepped straight into Henrik. His arms came out to balance them both. The heat of him around her had her breath snapping off. What was it about him that she couldn't resist? Her head was screaming at her to take three steps back, quick smart. But her heart, as usual, was over-ruling the situation.

"Forget something?" Henrik's voice floated around her. His hands found hers before breaking away. At least one of them seemed to have strength.

"Sorry. I forgot my coat."

Eva expected Henrik to send one of his burly body-guards to go get it and was surprised when he himself turned and jogged back to the car. Watching his lengthy form, she felt an additional shot of lust rush through her. He had a hold on her that she couldn't shake.

Taking a much-needed calming breath, she jogged on the spot to keep warm. Small puffs of air floated in front of her face.

The car park exit led onto a quiet street, but she could hear the bustling sounds of markets. Using the short reprieve on her senses, she looked about the area. The street was tree-lined, though bare of leaves at present. Wide streets were sandwiched by bike paths. She'd noticed more people chose to ride around as opposed to using cars here. It was eye opening to see the differences between Geravia and London. London was her home, had been ever since her gramps had taken her from Australia to the United Kingdom and claimed her as family. But something about this country was drawing her in, making her wish she could stay.

Eva didn't have a lot of memories of her parents, of her early years. The one clear image was of her mother quietly hand stitching away on a quilt, that eventually ended up on Eva's bed. The thought gave Eva pause, where had that quilt ended up? There hadn't been much left for her to take when her gramps had saved her.

"Earth to Eva?"

Starting, she turned to his voice. "Sorry, I was a million miles away."

"Care to share?" His blue eyes held concern.

"I was thinking about a quilt actually. One my mum made." They'd never touched on family during their short affair. On her requested terms, they'd not spoken of anything too personal. She'd made it so easy for him, making that rule. He wouldn't have wanted to share detailed family history with her; she had been nothing but a week of fun. Part of his 'week off' from royal life.

"Do your parents live in London?"

It was that question that really hit home on how little they knew about each other. Her parents were dead. Long gone, and he didn't even know that small fact about her. It wasn't even a big detail. More of her life was lived without her parents than with them. Why did his question grate so much?

Eva threaded her arms into the coat Henrik was holding up, turning her back towards him. "No, they don't."

Henrik's hands stayed on her shoulders for a moment, then spun her around to face him. His eyes were questioning. "What are you hiding behind those enchanting eyes?"

She opened her mouth to tell him, then shut it again. Lifting one shoulder slightly she offered a shrug, avoiding his seeking eyes.

"You shouldn't say things like that," she whispered the words, waiting for him to comment. His demeanour was certainly different today, which surprised Eva. She'd expected him to be standoffish. Instead, it appeared he really was making an effort at friendship.

"You're right. I shouldn't. Let's go check out these markets." He pointed to a small path Eva hadn't noticed. Nodding, she led the way. An uneasy silence stretched between them, but Eva couldn't be bothered to breach it.

The path led between towering buildings. Their shadows cast over the walkway left her icy cold. Eva pulled her coat tighter about herself. She was glad it didn't appear to be a long walk. The smell of roasting chestnuts assaulted her as they neared the end, causing a subconscious quickening of her steps.

Exiting the pathway, it felt like she'd entered another

world. People swarmed about, a hive of activity alongside the river. It appeared the markets were mainly food-related, interspersed with the occasional trinket stall. It was alive with every colour of the rainbow. Scanning her eyes around, she zeroed in on the source of the nutty scent. It reminded her of home, offering a safe haven from her topsy-turvy thoughts.

She grabbed Henrik's hand before dashing to join the queue that formed before the stall. The bright red umbrella canopy looked as if it would be more at home on a sunny sandy beach than in this dreary weather. It perked her mood immediately.

"You like chestnuts?"

"Who doesn't like roasted chestnuts?"

"Actually, me."

"You have tragic taste."

"No, I don't!" Mock outrage flashed on his face.

"Yeah, you do. Your taste buds must shudder on a daily basis."

"My taste buds are perfectly satisfied. Thank you for your concern."

Their childish conversation added to the lightness she felt inside. She'd been worried about today, about being in such close proximity to Henrik, but she needn't have. They were surrounded by people, not least of all his bodyguards, who stood out like sore thumbs in the casual, relaxed atmosphere. She didn't think the cap Henrik had donned would do him much good with the men in black standing nearby in stoic fashion, their presence alone signalling he was someone of interest.

Eva was amazed they lasted the five minutes it took her to reach the front of the line. Placing her order, she was trumped by Henrik stepping half across her to pay. Huffing in protest, the noise was washed aside as the server squeaked in recognition. Eva took a few quiet steps out of the way, abandoning Henrik to the lady's adoration. It was the first time she'd ever seen Henrik look embarrassed. Normally he was so sure of himself, so composed. But in the face of an ageing mum of three, if her tireless words were to be believed, he seemed to struggle to accept the praise she was showering over him.

It set the tone for the rest of their trip to the markets. They wandered down the strip, Eva occasionally ducking off to look at this and that. Henrik was constantly stopped, never complaining at the interruptions. Spying an ice-cream vendor at the end of the row, devoid of customers due to the cold, she moved past the current crowd around Henrik. She knew she'd regret the decision to buy ice cream when her teeth would be chattering halfway through her first bite, but she couldn't resist. Choosing a flavour was a struggle, settling on the chocolatey swirled concoction that promised hints of bourbon and cinnamon.

Returning to Henrik's side, she licked at the generous serving. Flavour burst on her tongue and she had to hide a moan.

"You look like you're enjoying that." Henrik's grin slid into place, making her realise her error.

"Sorry, I didn't even offer to get you one! That was thoughtless of me. I can go back ..."

"No. Thank you." He started walking, indicating a side street that led away from the markets. They'd reached the end of the row of vendors, leaving Eva to wonder where they were headed to next.

"Would you like a bite of mine?" She proffered the cone in his direction.

He raised an eyebrow. A small lift at the side of his mouth showed his humour. "I'll pass, thank you."

"You don't like ice cream?" She asked the question, leaving out the word 'anymore'. She didn't think it would be wise to make any further references to their time together in Italy.

Henrik coughed into his hand. "Yes, I like ice cream. As you already know. I just don't think I should take a lick of yours." His eyes caught hers. Heat flashed in his before his eyelashes shuttered down, his feelings concealed once more.

"Oh." She didn't really have an answer to that. "Where to next? Or do you have to get back to the palace?" Her words were spoken quickly, falling over themselves as she rushed to change the subject.

"No, not just yet. I have something else to show you, something I think you'll really enjoy."

"That sounds mysterious. You won't give me even a hint?"

"Nope. It's a surprise."

"Can I guess?"

"If you must. It's only a short walk so you'll need to be quick."

"Hmm. More markets?"

"No."

"A museum?"

"Not quite. But close. Here we are."

"Wow, you weren't kidding when you said, 'short walk'."

Henrik shook his head slightly at the closest bodyguard before opening the glass-fronted door for Eva to step through. She'd been distracted and hadn't looked at the building they'd arrived at but could see it was large. Warmth met her as they stepped inside.

"Let me take your coat." Henrik moved behind her. His

strong fingers brushed at her shoulders before she shrugged, allowing the coat to slide down her arms into his waiting grasp. Crisp footsteps sounded from behind her.

"Prince Henrik, it's our honour to see you back so soon." An older gentleman dressed in a burgundy uniform stopped before them, bowing deeply.

"Thank you, George. Please let me introduce Miss Eva James, a designer from London. Is the exhibition ready? I had Stefan call earlier to arrange for a private viewing."

"Of course, Your Highness. This way please. It's our pleasure to have you attend the Geravia Meusae, Miss James. It'll be wonderful to hear any feedback you have. Are you a couture designer yourself?"

Couture? Eva's heart skipped at the word.

George ushered them through an arched doorway, red velvet drapes tied back at its edges. Eva couldn't stop the gasp that escaped at the sight before her.

"That's ..." *Breath-taking.* Too enchanted by the gowns before her, she froze, her next words and answer to the question put to her fading in her mind. On autopilot, she moved to stand before the row of dresses. They were placed on pure white mannequins staged in different poses, each gown dripping with beauty and hours of work. Beading, embroidery, pleating, silk, tulle... her head catalogued everything. Her mouth hung open, unable to contain the giddy excitement of being so close to some of the world's most famous and fabulous haute couture designs.

They'd been arranged in colour variation, each accompanied by a short script from the designer. Dior, Valentino, Chanel. She spotted an older Elsa Schiaparelli gown she remembered drooling over in one of her books from her time at design school. The design was deceptive, looked so simple, when she knew it must have taken hours to get the cut and drape just right to achieve such a divine silhouette.

She sensed more than heard Henrik come and stand beside her.

"It's been a long collaboration to get this ready. It won't open to the public for another two weeks, but I requested a special pass to come show you. I'm on the board."

The words filtered in slowly, her pleasure at the designs before her overtaken by the thoughtful gesture. She spun towards him, launching her arms around his neck. It wasn't appropriate but she simply didn't care. "Thank you. This is just ... thank you."

Her grin was wider than a kid left unattended in a candy store. She flitted about the exhibition, peering closely at the minute details: the decadent over-embellishment, the hours of hand stitching and carefully chosen beads and sequins. Reading the notes, she marvelled at one dress which had required more than 2,500 hours of sewing, involving a team of seamstresses and thousands of Swarovski crystals and pearls.

She held in a squeal when she reached an original Charles James gown. The style appeared to be from the fifties, the description plate confirming her thoughts. She brought to mind a famous image of Charles James' gowns, beautiful women lazily propped about, decked out in elegant fashion. That one image had prompted her initial dreams of designing. A framed copy still sat in her drawer back home, a gift from her gramps. It wouldn't be worth anything, but to her it was priceless.

A frown took over her features, knitting her brows together slightly. Today seemed to be a day of memories firing at her from all directions.

"Is something the matter?"

She turned to the voice, having forgotten Henrik. He'd left her to roam and she had assumed he'd gone off to sit somewhere whilst she ran about exploring.

"No, gosh no. How could anything be the matter? This is like dying and arriving at fashion heaven. I've seen so many of these dresses in books, images of them on websites—I never dreamed I'd get to see so many of them in real life. Be close enough to touch them." Her voice sounded wistful and dreamy, childlike in its reverence and enthusiasm. This was one of the most thoughtful things anyone had ever done for her; she could kiss Henrik she was so thankful to him.

Or maybe she just wanted to kiss him.

"Come this way. I'll show you my favourite."

Eva's spell was broken at Henrik's words; she hadn't expected him to have any interest in the exhibition, never mind a favourite gown. She accepted the proffered hand. His smooth palm accelerated her already pumping heart. The thought that she shouldn't be taking his hand was quickly discarded. Today was not the day for regrets or considering the things she should not be doing. Today she would just let herself enjoy.

They walked through two expansive rooms filled with glittering outfits and a selection of shoes before reaching a small alcove. The room was round, with dimmed lighting and a soft lilting song playing in the background. Eva struggled to place the music. The memory of hearing it before drifted on the side of her subconscious but wouldn't quite slip into focus.

Unlike the other dresses, this was laid out flat on a marble stone block. Eva could tell it was beautiful. It was a rich blue, with a long skirt created by yards of fabric from what she could tell. She stepped closer until she stood over the top. The volume of the skirt had hidden details from her view but now, she could see clearly. It was another Charles James gown. The folds of fabric, the lines of the design, were all exquisite.

"It was a gift to my mum from my father. He had crown jewels designed specifically to match the rich blue, sapphires and diamonds. It was her favourite dress."

Henrik spoke the words as if from far away, in his own memories. She could see pain on his features, etched into frown lines she wasn't sure he even knew he was making. Her hand squeezed his, reminding him of their connection, of her support. There was a mystery that seemed to surround the queen's death. Eva wanted to ask what had happened, how the queen had died, but sensed now wouldn't be the right time.

"That's very generous, including this gown that must be so precious to your family as part of the exhibition. I'm sure it will be the highlight. It certainly has been for me."

Henrik shrugged a shoulder slightly, still not looking directly at her. She studied his profile, his face rid of all signs of pain. They were replaced by a mask free of expression. His stature was ramrod straight, like he was on display, saluting at a public event. He was back to being unreachable.

Eva removed her hand. The hold they were sharing had lost its value. She berated her folly for thinking this outing meant more than it really did. Henrik himself had told her yesterday he was simply carrying out a duty for his brother. Not in any way the romantic date that she had turned it into thanks to her fanciful thoughts and dreams.

Henrik felt bereft the moment her hand left his. He was

thankful she had some sense though; he was getting too close again. Today wasn't meant to be a walk down Memory Lane, but that was how it had turned out.

"I thought you'd appreciate the value of this exhibition."

"It's amazing Henrik, truly."

"I've been through the whole exhibit a few times. I like to be involved, particularly given some of the items are my families. It was actually my father who suggested we add this dress of my mother's. I hadn't realised he'd even kept it."

Henrik felt lost in his memory, the dress bringing him too close to memories of the mother he'd so suddenly lost.

Eva looked at him, her eyes offering support and comfort he didn't deserve. It was that look that kept him talking.

"I can recall seeing my mother in this dress a handful of times. It's not the done thing, but my mother never cared to wear new outfits at every occasion; she just wore what she loved. This dress... God she loved it. It just brought her to life."

"Maybe it made her feel comfortable. I would imagine being queen could be quite nerve-wracking. Wearing something she loved and obviously suited her would have helped."

Henrik had never considered that angle before. He'd been such a blind fool to this mother's inner emotional workings, she'd hidden them so well. That's why her death had been such a shock. But Eva's words now made so much sense.

"I remember creeping out of the nursery when I was younger, at Izzie's request. Even then she was a force to be reckoned with, begging me to sneak her out to look at the annual charity ball. I was ten, so Izzie would have been six. I can still recall every blunt word of my father's dressing down at my irresponsible behaviour, but it had been worth the tirade to see my mother's face lit with such joy. She'd sparkled with happiness, her glow outshining all those around her. Father had looked regal, but his eyes had changed whenever they'd met hers. True love—it was evident to all those who'd been there."

"What a beautiful memory. I bet Izzie has never forgotten you doing that for her."

"Possibly. We don't talk about our mother. I do remember Izzie's squeal of delight at seeing all the women dressed up in tiara's. She'd been a six-year-old princess, wishing away the years so she herself could attend." Eva's eyes widened, concern entering their whiskey depths at his words regarding his mother. This would be the perfect time to tell her, to explain what had happened to his mother and why he hadn't turned up in Italy. His chest clenched at the thought of dredging up those memories.

"My mother wasn't born into royalty; in fact she wasn't even born middle class. She'd been a very poor student, on holidays backpacking across Europe when she'd stumbled upon my father. At first, she hadn't wanted anything to do with him when she found out he was going to be a king, but that hadn't stopped him pursuing her."

"That sounds kind of familiar." Eva smiled and he could tell she was trying to lighten the mood. Did she sense that this tale didn't have a happy ending? Much like theirs didn't, but at least he was safe in the knowledge that pushing her away would save her from suffering the same fate at his mother.

"It does a little." He offered a half-smile, but it didn't reach his eyes, he was too lost in his memories of his mother, of how he'd missed the signs of her unhappiness. "It was a big change for my mother. My grandfather passed a week after my parents wedding, throwing them into the roles of king and queen. I remember my mother speaking of her shock at being thrown into such a position, she said she'd barely settled into the role of wife and princess, and already hated the media intrusion on her life. Then suddenly, she was a queen. It was one of the few times she'd looked unsure of herself ... I should have realised then that something was wrong."

"Henrik, what happened to your mother?"

His heart splintered at the look within her eyes, like she wanted to take his pain away and he hadn't even told her the truth. He opened his mouth to tell her everything but at the last moment his guilt made him change his words. He could have saved his mother, and he wasn't ready to tell the woman who stood before him, so pure and untainted by his world, the full truth.

"She died. The circumstances ... were a bit suspicious but it was ruled an accident. They found her in her wisteria pergola. There wasn't anything they could do."

Her gasp reached the depths of his soul. He turned away, his eyes hot and itchy, but he refused to acknowledge the feeling, slamming his emotions away.

He could feel Eva's eyes on him, sensing that she wanted to reach out. He was thankful that she read him well enough not to ask for more details.

"I'm so sorry, Henrik."

He heard her swallow. Silence stretched for what felt like eternity but in reality, was probably only half a minute, before she continued. "Thank you for sharing this exhibit with me. I imagine it will be a huge success."

He grasped the subject change like a lifeline.

"Thank you. Izzie pitched in to help a lot; it has been good for her to have a focus. I hope she'll take over my place on the board once I'm ..." *Married.* He thought the word more than said it, not wanting to bring up Sophia just now. So much of him wished life were different, that he were born just a common man, free to love who he chose. Well, he was free to love who he chose, he supposed, but it wouldn't be fair to Eva.

She seemed to be handling the media and being in the spotlight just fine now ... but who was to say that would last? His mother had seemed to be fine too ... but looks were deceiving. His wife would be under a lot of pressure; Sophia was used to that. The country needed stability in its monarchy.

"Would you like to try it on?"

The words slipped out before he could sensor them. Why the heck had he suggested that?

The wistful look of excitement on Eva's face wiped any remorse he felt at offering. "This dress? It's priceless... Are you sure?" Uncertainty danced across her face, but her brown eyes were lit with elation.

"Sure. Just let me arrange a space for you." He beckoned Frank forward, indicating he needed the museum director back. A few quick directions and an area was found for Eva to dress, mirrors from another exhibition provided, and an assistant was secured to help her into the dress. It was all very quick and efficient—exactly what he'd asked for and was used to.

Eva had looked a little unsure as she followed the assistant to the makeshift changeroom, fidgeting with the bracelet on her slim wrist. He'd noticed she still wore it constantly, but neither had mentioned its origin again. He was really making an impossible situation worse but couldn't stop himself. Seeing the delight on her face was becoming an addiction. Being close to her, breathing her same air, was helping him breathe properly in situations he hadn't realised he was struggling with. Eva was his proverbial breath of fresh air.

Five years ago, he'd walked away with no explanation and no excuses. Simply vanished from her life and he'd felt like a cad ever since. He had to find a way to be completely honest with her. It wouldn't change how he felt towards marriage, and marry he must, but it might help provide closure to them both on these feelings that crackled as strongly today as they did that moment they'd first met.

He fished out his phone from his pocket, checking the schedule Stefan emailed him on a daily basis. He'd had the morning cleared, but this afternoon he had a board meeting, then a cocktail engagement. Flicking Stefan a quick text, he requested he cancel this evening's appointment. They wouldn't miss him. Stefan's response was a carefully worded rebuke on his decision, but Henrik chose to ignore it. For once he was putting himself first, to make a decision with himself in mind, not the country.

A nervous cough caught his attention. Eva let out a giggle as she twirled on the spot, holding out the side folds of the dress. Words assaulted his mind: delightful, exquisite, beautiful ... she was illuminated with happiness from within. Henrik wanted nothing more than to sweep her into his arms and kiss her, never letting her go. The silk of the dress rustled to a stop, smoothed into place by Eva's palms.

His mind snapped the image—her standing before him swathed in regal blue, her hair whisped up into a loose chignon, her eyes fresh with excitement. Eva's face shone with the same beauty and innocence his mother's had at the ball, though she had been quite a few years older than Eva was now when she wore the dress.

The thought caught his heart and squeezed. He struggled to breathe through the comparison. A man with sickly pale skin looked back at him in the mirror. Was that him?

"Are you okay? I'm sorry. I shouldn't have tried it on." Eva's face became a picture of concern, worry etched in her eyes.

"No. You look beautiful. Apologies, I just remembered I have something to attend to." He was such an idiot. He needed to find a way to walk away from Eva, to stop inviting her further into his heart. "I'll have one of my bodyguards escort you home. Take your time at the exhibition." With that he turned on his heel and fled. He needed to find space to breathe again, resurrect the wall inside. Seeing Eva just now made him realise he hadn't fully dealt with his feelings surrounding his mother's death. So much of him felt responsible, that if he'd just accepted his role of first born and been happy in that position, he'd have realised she was struggling. He'd have been here to talk to her and perhaps she'd still be alive today.

13

Eva was surprised to receive the note from Henrik asking her to join him for dinner. It was handwritten, for one thing, which was quite sweet. He'd all but run from the exhibition room, leaving Eva unsure as to what she'd done wrong. Perhaps it wasn't so much her, but his mother's dress. He'd gone a pasty shade of white when he'd looked up to see her in it. She should have said no, especially after what he'd just told her about his mother, how it was her favourite dress. Seeing it on anyone else would probably give him mixed feelings.

It had been an honour for Eva to see the dress so close, never mind trying it on. She'd really felt like a princess in it, which was silly, but it was like something out of a fairy tale or a romance novel. Not real life.

She hadn't hung around after Henrik's departure. After carefully changing back into her own clothes, she'd gingerly returned the dress to the assistant, letting her rearrange it in its solo room. It was almost sad that it was locked in a room by itself, like the passing of the queen still cast a shadow over the country. Eva still felt like there was more to that story than Henrik had told her.

An odd thought to have really. Fingering the textured parchment of the note, she read it again, deciding she had time to do a bit of quick research before getting ready. She didn't want to dwell too much on Henrik's short apology and request to dine together tonight.

Throwing her scarf on the corner armchair, she continued through to her work room. Izzie's dress sat proudly in the corner; it was finished but for a final fitting and hem check. She needed to see when Izzie was free. Really, she should have been doing that today, not gallivanting around with a prince. Someone else's prince. Someone else's fiancé. God, she'd been an idiot to think that today was some sort of date. She was finding herself more and more confused. She needed to just finish her time here then get the hell out of the country.

Taking a seat, she tapped in her password and brought up a search page. The cursor flickered at her, waiting for her to find the right words. 'Queen Margot of Stenaco' brought up images of an extremely elegant woman, and stories about her charity work and her wedding to King Bastian. 'Fairy tale romance' seemed to be one of the most popular headlines. Flicking through a couple, she found a few with images of the couple with their children, plus some birth announcements and royal family photos.

Eva added the word 'death' to her original search. The first was an official announcement from the palace, stating that it was a sudden illness and that the family would appreciate being left to grieve in peace.

After that, the tone changed. There were speculations on the death not being illness, and the media hounding the family for the real story. Stenaco was a country in mourning and was losing faith in the royal family.

Eva shut the lid on her laptop. She felt intrusive searching the royal family, particularly whilst staying in the palace as a guest. What had really happened with the queen? No wonder no one seemed to talk about her. It sounded like a dreadful time for everyone involved.

Attempting to put the search out of her mind, she picked up the note again from Henrik. Why did he want to have dinner with her? His actions had her spinning in circles, along with her reactions.

She groaned aloud at that thought, *kisses ... plural.* Not just one kiss, one slip—there had been two. What was she thinking of, kissing Henrik, an engaged man? So, they had a past, a strong connection that didn't appear to have lessened with time for either of them, but that didn't give her the right to go around kissing him. Or, more correctly, for him to go around kissing her! Frustration built at the thought. Why was she letting this go on? Why wasn't she demanding answers, like she'd originally wanted to?

It was time to get back on track, thank Henrik for a lovely day, cross a line through their past and move forward —once and for all.

In the end, it hadn't taken Eva long to get ready. She'd selected a dress from those that Felix had put in her walk-in, hoping to use it as a reminder as to why she was at the palace, why she was in Geravia. It was cream silk, very demure, sheer at the sleeves and across the top. The bodice was fitted, the skirt flaring to a slight A-line which floated nicely if she twirled. Not that she'd be twirling; it wasn't like Henrik would ask her to dance. Oh, she had to stop! Her brain was running haywire on the ideas of what tonight was going to bring, why he'd asked her to dinner. It was driving her batty.

She left her hair loose, brushing out the length until it hung in straight glossy strands to her shoulders. Choosing only her bracelet for jewellery, she left the walk-in before she could change her mind on her outfit or going at all.

Her heels bounced slightly on the carpeted floor as she walked towards the back-garden terrace. She hadn't been at the palace long, but thankfully, it was long enough to have worked out where everything was situated. Well, the main areas anyway. She still hadn't worked out where the kitchen was and was kind of missing the simple task of just making herself breakfast.

Henrik stood waiting on the terrace when she arrived, his back to her. She took the chance to study his broad shoulders, clad in a black suit jacket. The sun was dipping in the sky, almost disappearing from view, leaving in its place a golden glow amidst pink- and purple-hued clouds. The air was brisk, she should have brought a shawl or coat to keep herself warm. Spotting the heat lamp set up next to an intimate dinner setting, she breathed a sigh of relief.

After stepping through the glass French doors, she closed them with a soft click. Henrik spun in her direction.

"Hi." Eva cringed inwardly at her awkward greeting. Nervousness had erupted within her with every step she'd taken towards the dinner.

"Thanks for coming, Eva. I wasn't sure you would after my behaviour today. I'm sorry for leaving so suddenly, I just needed some time to think a few things over."

Eva was surprised by Henrik's admission—even more so when he walked over to her before taking her hand and leading her to the table setting. The whole set-up was a picture of romance, complete with luscious mauve-coloured roses set in crystal taking centre stage on the table. Eva took the seat Henrik held out for her, enjoying the mix of his aftershave mingling with the rich smell of the roses.

Uncertainty crept in, her thoughts from earlier demanding answers.

"Henrik, what's going on? Why dinner?"

His face broke into a smile; a cheeky glint lit his eyes. Eva responded by narrowing her gaze at him. She wanted answers, not some game.

"I'm sorry. It's just that's the first time you've addressed me as Henrik, without any formal crap beforehand."

"That's not true!" Was it? Or was it ...

The situation between them tonight did feel different. She'd come to dinner to gain answers from their time in Italy ... his being a prince was something he'd left out, but for some reason, she couldn't summon any anger at his lying to her about that anymore. The man in Italy, the prince here, were both the same. There were some key differences in their behaviour for sure ... but so many reasons why she loved him, was still in love with him, hadn't changed. Her stomach lurched at the thought. How could she still be in love with him? When had that happened? How had she let herself fall all over again, especially now she knew the whole truth about who he was and how hopeless their situation was. Her heart still betrayed her, still sought nothing but to be broken into a million pieces. Again.

Her breath huffed out, causing a little puff of cold air to dance into the evening sky.

"Are you cold? The heater's on but I can arrange for a shawl or blanket for you?"

"I just want some answers." Frustration at herself showed

in her voice. She was a fool to have fallen for Henrik again, but no way would she walk away tonight until she got the truth. She deserved that much. "I feel like we've been dancing around this since I arrived. I can't pretend I'm happy to just ignore our time in Italy anymore. You've kissed me, twice! I think I deserve some clarification, don't you? You're meant to be engaged!"

At her mention of kissing, his eyes dipped briefly to her lips, desire flashing in their depths before the emotion was wiped away by a slight flinch.

"You're right. You deserve answers, and that's why I asked you to dinner. But can I please ask that you let the chef serve the entrées first at least? She's made some special Stenish dishes. I thought you'd enjoy them."

She tried to not roll her eyes, she really did, but his laugh told her she'd failed to conceal the movement. "Sure, let's eat."

The entrée was delicious, trussed quails nestled within pickled vegetables. The vegetables had been thinly sliced and coiled, the different colours popping amid micro herbs and edible flowers. Part of Eva didn't want to eat it, it looked so pretty on the plate. The chef had certainly gone to a lot of trouble with presentation.

Henrik poured them both generous glasses of a crisp-looking white, its clear visage deceptive compared to the punch of flavour that burst on her tongue when she took her first sip. It enhanced the flavour of the quail beautifully. Eva wanted to ask where the wine was from but didn't want to encourage a new line of questioning until she got answers to her original questions.

"I missed a call, the night before we were to meet. In Italy. It was from my mother. She left me a voicemail which I'd ignored."

Eva had been in the process of gathering up one of the last bites on her plate when Henrik's quiet words broke the silence. His eyes were downcast, gazing at his empty plate. Not sure if he was planning to continue, Eva put her last bite in her mouth. What had been full of flavour before now could have been cardboard for all she could taste. She chewed methodically, waiting for more words.

"I want you to know I never planned to stand you up that next night. I was about to leave when my father called, telling me I needed to come home. My mother was in hospital. She'd tried to take her own life. They'd found her in her rose garden. That's why I don't like going there."

Eva elicited a shocked gasp, her thoughts diving in a million different directions.

Henrik took a deep swallow from his wine glass. He refilled it, sloshing in the liquid before topping up her mostly untouched glass. He set the bottle back into the ice bucket, spinning it until the label was displayed. She'd never seen him fuss so much before, and realised he was stalling.

"She died before I arrived home. Afterwards the palace issued a statement saying she'd passed away from a sudden illness. I didn't agree with lying to the public, but our father was devastated, struggling to function, and it was decided it would be less scandalous to run with that story than the truth.

"Unfortunately, a month after her death, after thousands of citizens attended her funeral, a story broke with the truth. One of the hospital staff accepted a bribe from the media. We denied the story, but the media wouldn't let it go. It caused havoc throughout the country and we lost a lot of support."

Eva felt sick. Henrik was telling her the truth; she'd only today read articles speculating on this.

"I put all my focus into building back that support. Helping father repair relations and putting on a united front. I was grieving and by the time I felt even the tiniest bit normal again, I didn't know how I could bring myself to contact you."

Eva's heart hurt. Her whole body hurt. She wanted to cry for the man who'd lost his mother, to have to experience such intrusion in a deeply personal time. She wanted to cry at the injustice of timing. Part of her brain had to question why he hadn't been able to track her down with such means at his fingertips, but she snuffed out the thought. It didn't help her to play the *what if* game; she'd dedicated too many hours of her life to that just after she'd arrived home from Italy.

"I'm so sorry about your mother. I understand why you didn't contact me now and I appreciate the truth. I won't lie and say it hasn't been something I've always wondered about." Eva ached to reach out and touch Henrik, place a connection between them, but she didn't know how.

"I wish things had been different, Eva—that I'd been able to meet you that night, to tell you of my feelings. I hadn't wanted our relationship to end that way, or at all. But as you can see, this is my life: I am the crown prince of Stenaco, and will be crowned king one day. I have a lot of expectation placed on me, and my wife will need to meet those expectations too, will be required to give up her life for that. Give up her freedom. Sophia understands those sacrifices." Henrik was saying one thing, but his eyes were telling another story. He was offering an apology. Telling her without words that she wasn't up to the task of being his wife, would likely never have been. She wanted so much to tell him differently, that she'd do whatever it took to prove she was up to the role of wife and queen, that their love for each other would be enough.

But would it?

She had absolutely no experience with royalty, with how to act in front of the media, at state events. She came with no pedigree, no money. She'd toyed with the limelight for a few weeks, and whilst it hadn't been terrible, she had come to realise how little privacy the royals really got when it came to living their lives. The majority of their time was scheduled, booked into meetings and dinners.

Not to mention the media. Prior to this trip Eva hadn't paid any attention to social media. Now she found herself checking in regularly, seeing what people said about her. And some of it hurt a lot. How much worse would that be if she was really involved with Henrik instead of fake dating Felix?

She selected one of the roses from the vase, plucking it out and burying her nose in its fragrance, hoping to hide the awful feelings of loss that accompanied Henrik's statement. She hadn't realised until this point that she'd still held some kind of hope he was inviting her to dinner tonight to confess he still loved her, like she loved him.

Henrik cleared his throat, capturing her attention. "I'm sorry Felix had to go away. Are you missing him?"

It was the first time he'd directly asked about her supposed relationship with Felix. Other than that first kiss, it really had been a lame attempt at a pretend relationship. She'd been seen with him at many events, but without that initial fake kiss they could just be close friends. Did Henrik suspect as much? The way he was scrutinising her made her think he was looking in the right direction, that her supposed feelings were fake.

Nerves raced around her body like mice on a wheel. Felix hadn't said she had to keep their deal a secret, but it was kind of assumed, right? Or should she come clean? Tell Henrik she was being paid to pretend ... that thought didn't sit well. She wanted to tell him the truth. She was sitting here having an intimate romantic dinner with Henrik when she was supposed to be dating his brother. She was lying to him. Though he was the one engaged ... did that make her sin the lesser one?

Caught in a slight spin of panic, she clutched for her wine glass, in the process knocking it flying. The pale-yellow liquid flew across the table, splattering the tablecloth and reaching the pristine white of Henrik's shirt. She figured she'd find his yelp comical another time, but right then she was horrified.

"Oh, my goodness! Sorry!" Jumping from her chair, she snatched at the napkin she'd earlier placed across her lap. Without thought, she grabbed a handful of Henrik's shirt, blotting at the damp, discoloured fabric. "Is this silk? It should probably be sent to the cleaner's straight away so it doesn't stain." Her fingers brushed warm skin. Rock-hard warm skin, immediately robbing her of her next words, her next breath. Her skin prickled, realising Henrik had gone really still. She ordered herself not to look up, to just drop the shirt from her grasp and walk away.

She'd never been good at following her own orders.

Her eyes crept up slowly, noting the matte polish on the tiny silver stud buttons. The fine stitching lines that ran the length of the button placket, ending with the top button undone. A fine dusting of hair peeked from that top crevice, her fingers following the path with a mind of their own.

"Eva ..."

Her name was a whisper on his breath, and she knew

she was lost. *They* were lost. She waited for the kiss she knew was coming, could feel his breath at her cheek as he gently caressed it with his lips. Slight stubble rubbed against her smooth skin, eliciting a sigh of pleasure at the contact. She blocked out thoughts of her deal with Felix, of Henrik all but admitting he was marrying to help his country, not for his heart. All thoughts of their previous lost love melted into a need to be together right now.

"I've never forgotten you." His words wrapped around her.

"Nor I you." Her eyes met his, melting in the love that she saw there. "I love you. I loved you then, and it seems I've fallen for you all over again. Felix and I ... it's all been a ruse—"

His finger pressed against her lips.

She'd ached to be in Henrik's arms again, to feel this essential rightness. She knew without a doubt that they belonged together; she just needed to find a way to prove that to Henrik. To show him their love mattered above all else.

Soft, delicious lips replaced his finger. It felt like coming home. This kiss was different to the others, it was honest and passionate and raw. She let out a soft cry when his lips broke away from hers, hovering barely an inch away to whisper his next words.

"I love you too."

14

———

*H*enrik surfaced from a delicious dream, one he soon realised wasn't a dream, but real life. Euphoria swept through him, holding Eva's naked form against his length. She still loved him; she'd whispered the words to him again during their lovemaking the night before. And it had been lovemaking. Never had he thought he'd feel such happiness again, such a sense of contentment as he had with her in his arms.

He stroked the petal-soft skin at her hip before placing a gentle kiss on her shoulder. It was still dark out, and he needed to return to his room. It was one thing for his closest bodyguards to know where he'd spent the night; he didn't want to advertise the fact to the whole palace staff until he'd spoken with Felix. He needed to speak to Sophia too, though she'd been daily encouraging him to sort out his true feelings for Eva, and had all but excused herself from their agreement.

There was still so much to be said between Eva and him, but he was sure they would work it out. Felix's motives still niggled at him, but she'd confessed her love—he knew she'd meant every word. There was no guile in Eva. She said what she meant. Her honesty was something he loved about her.

Quietly slipping from the warmth, the cold air had him wishing he could dive straight back under the covers, wake Eva with a proper good morning kiss. But he needed to be sensible about the situation, put Eva's modesty first. The palace staff were paid highly and signed waivers to keep their mouths shut, but that hadn't stopped them before.

Eva shifted slightly, murmuring his name before her breathing evened out again. Quickly stepping into his dress pants, he slid his arms into the stained shirt, a smile lighting his face at the memory. That wine was now his all-time favourite; he'd have to see if Eva would be okay with him arranging to have cases shipped in especially for their wedding. It could be their own private joke. Now he was getting ahead of himself.

The corridor was empty when he slipped out, the thick carpet masking his steps back towards his rooms. Walking past one of the windows, he caught a glimpse of the rose garden basking in the moonlight. It was a serene picture, and for once he didn't feel sad when he looked at it. In fact, he realised he felt a sense of freedom, of possibility. Eva had done that. Having her here helped free him from the constraints that were strangling his life.

He hoped she'd choose him. Choose a life with him. It would be hard, but he'd be there, holding her hand. Reaching his rooms, he decided he'd slept enough; his body was buzzing with energy that needed a release. Checking the time—four thirty a.m.—he discarded the idea of the gym, instead deciding upon a swim. The water would douse his excess energy in no time.

Twenty continuous laps later, the water sloshing through his fingers, he realised that whilst he was puffed, energy still coursed through him. He needed to make plans.

He could arrange a breakfast picnic, leave a note under Eva's door for her to meet him in the wisteria centre of the garden. He wanted to make new memories, wash away all previous thoughts of what had happened there. He smiled at the idea. Surely, she'd like that. He'd bring blankets to ward off the cold morning air.

Pulling his body from the water he sat on the edge of the pool, filling his lungs with deep breaths as droplets slicked down his torso.

"Henrik! Thank goodness I've found you. You need to see this."

Stefan's voice was panicked, an unwelcome intrusion on his delighted thoughts. It took a lot to panic Stefan, and if his face was anything to go by, something terrible had happened.

Henrik's gaze narrowed on the newspaper Stefan clutched. Henrik stood, grabbing his robe and pulling it on before Stefan arrived before him, thrusting out the paper like it was covered in poison.

Not covered—*filled*. Bile rose in Henrik's mouth as he read the headline. "Dammit!" Anger coursed through him, vibrating through every part of his body.

"How did this get through the press office? Why weren't we warned this article would run?"

Anger turned to hopelessness. His earlier delight was now tainted. He should have connected the dots sooner. The media had been all over the story that Eva and Felix were rumoured to be dating. But where had they found images of him and Eva so close?

"I need to go see her."

"I asked the same question of the press secretary. It seems the original story ran in a London tabloid late last night. This particular paper has been itching to break the rules on going through the palace on any gossip articles not officially confirmed by the press office. They've found a loophole and have chosen today to use it. Do I need to have a response drafted?"

Henrik stopped his march at Stefan's question. The short answer was yes, but the longer one was more involved. What response would be best at this time? He needed to speak to Eva, double check she was okay, before anything was made public.

"Give me an hour."

The words from the article seared across his mind. *Twice the fun—which prince will win?* The headline was vile, playing on themes of rivalry that they'd tried to report on over the years between the brothers. He knew in a way there was some truth to the article. Eva had kissed his brother. He hadn't confirmed the full story with Eva last night, but she had said things between her and Felix were a ruse... They'd been going to talk through everything this morning.

He could hear Eva's voice through the door, even though it was shut. He stopped, wondering who it was she was talking to. The sound of Felix's voice, muffled through the oak wood, was a surprise. Felix was meant to be in Copenhagen; why was he back? Had he seen the article?

Leaning in closer, he was able to make out the gist of the conversation. A deal wasn't working out; Felix insisted Eva still take the money; Eva said she had to go home ... At the last part, Henrik lurched at the door handle, and bust through the door. All thoughts of the article, the situation, of anything but stopping her had disappeared from his mind.

The room went eerily quiet with his entrance. Felix was reclined in an armchair, one leg slung over the arm, his head propped up by one hand, the other clutching a large takeaway coffee. Eva had possibly been pacing, but had stopped, her face set.

"Brother, to what do we owe the honour?" Felix said lazily.

"I came to check on Eva. Why are you back?"

"Stefan sent some cryptic message saying it would be best if I came home. Something about an article?" Felix's brow raised in question, nodding at the paper being strangled in Henrik's grasp. "Is that it?"

"You haven't seen it then?" Henrik's voice was solemn, and he tried his best not to look Eva's way. His heart was screaming at him to look at her, move towards her, to offer some physical comfort before he had to reveal the paper. It was bad for him and his brother, but it painted her in the worst light, like she was a gold-digging whore willing to seduce either of the brothers into a royal position that would further her own fashion brand. There had even been a snide comment—*would the king be next?* He cringed at the poor wording, that he hadn't been able to protect Eva from this sort of gutter press.

He was living every nightmare he'd ever had with Eva being punished by his royal position. If he wasn't royalty, no one would even care.

Without a word, he passed the paper over to Eva. She stood with her arms folded, staring at the newspaper for a while before gingerly plucking it from his fingers. It appeared she was avoiding his gaze, for which he was thankful. Her gasp was like a knife to the heart. Her shoulders physically shrank into her body with every pass of her eyes across the front page. Her bottom lip began to tremble just as tears welled in her eyes, silently dripping down her face.

Eva was a picture of utter devastation. And it was his fault. He'd done this to her. if he'd just stayed away from her he could have saved her this heartache.

Last night had been magical, just like their time together in Italy all those years ago. But, like then, he was living in a dream bubble. Eva didn't deserve a life sentence, which was what being with him would be. His mother had told him he had to choose wisely when it came to a wife, and she'd been right.

He couldn't live his life with the possibility that Eva would be torn apart in the media. With the possibility she'd find it all too much and leave him. Or worse, take her life like his mother had.

He remembered the awful feeling of cold when he'd arrived back in Stenaco to be told his mother was dead. That she hadn't made it. He'd been too late to save her. His world had shattered at having his one true support line taken from him. Because of this life. Because of the pressures of palace life.

His gut churned at the thought, burning acid replacing the coffee he'd slugged down on his way to Eva's room. His veins filled with ice, knowing he needed to make the right decision, to end things with her before they'd even begun. Again. He would need to be brutal to make her leave, make her believe he held no love for her. But she was better off without him, better off if he stuck to the decision he'd made all those years ago after hearing his mum's voicemail. Eva deserved to live her life in freedom. She deserved someone better than him.

Eva couldn't speak, her body frozen with humiliation. Not only from the article—that was a pile of rubbish—but the images used to skew the truth. Worse was the way Henrik was avoiding her gaze. All signs of the love written on his face last night had disappeared. He was back behind his wall, and that scared Eva.

He'd left. Again.

Eva wasn't going to hang around to be made a fool of once more.

Waking this morning to an empty bed had been embarrassing to say the least. Fossicking back through her memories of the night before, she realised Henrik hadn't ever said he was planning to commit to her. He'd just implied he wasn't in a position to marry as he chose, that his marriage would be what was best for the country.

Looking at the paper in her hands, at the man she loved who wouldn't even look at her, she knew without a doubt she wasn't making the list of what was 'best' for the country. At this very moment, she was a laughingstock, smeared as nothing more than a promiscuous woman pitting the princes against one another.

Eva was glad she'd skipped breakfast, as she was pretty certain if she'd had it, it would be coming back up right now. Taking a step forward, she thrust the paper at Felix before moving to the breakfast tray set up in her room. Averting her eyes from the toast, she gulped back some water, hoping to wash away the bad taste in her mouth.

She heard Felix stand, exchanging heated words with Henrik. Her mind couldn't decipher the words; they were just a fuzzy blur of background noise. It didn't matter what the words were anyway. The damage had been done. If one paper had run the story, she could only imagine others would follow. Would it have made it to the London press by now?

A hand at her arm had her jumping, her skin burning from the contact. She was cold, shivering in fact. Was this shock? It must be.

She looked up at Henrik, then about the room. Felix had left. She felt odd, like she was watching this whole situation from somewhere else.

"Is there any way to stop the article? If it makes the London press it will kill my gramps' business." Was that her voice? She sounded like a lunatic, all rushed and panicked.

Henrik's face blanched, sympathy written across his features. "It was released first in London."

His words were like a second blow to the stomach. Reading the article in the Geravian press had been bad enough, but knowing it was already making the rounds back home? What would her gramps think?

She'd come to Stenaco to help save her gramps' business, and with one stupid article she'd probably damaged his reputation beyond repair. The money wouldn't matter if they had no clients—clients who placed integrity and privacy above all else.

Her day had gone from bad to worse. First, waking with Henrik gone, she'd started to second guess her position with him. He might have said he loved her, but not once had he said he'd call off his engagement to Sophia. Her deal with Felix was a farce and honestly, she didn't feel okay with pretending anymore. She'd told Felix she was considering leaving, not wanting to wait to hear Henrik tell her she wasn't good enough. She'd finished Izzie's dress enough for someone else to do the final fitting. There was no reason for her to be here. Now this?

"Eva, I think we made a mistake last night."

Eva wondered if she'd heard correctly, but looking up at Henrik, she knew she had. Stepping back, his hand dropped from her arm. Heat surged into her face along with more unwanted tears.

There were the words she'd been expecting.

Confirmation she just wasn't good enough, as she'd suspected all along.

This morning she'd been going to just quietly slip away, avoid this confrontation, but was it the right move now? She may not have had a title, or have palace training, but she'd been handling herself just fine this past few weeks. If Henrik really loved her, he'd fight for her.

"I really don't understand you, Henrik. One moment you're showing me your beautiful city, taking me to private couture showings, and making love to me ... the next, you're saying it's a mistake. Is there some law against you being with a commoner?"

"No."

"Then what the hell is the problem? If there's no law against it, what is holding you back? We love each other. Isn't that enough?

"No."

She physically stepped back, like distance would make that one word go away.

"I don't believe you."

"Then believe I need to marry someone who was born to this life. Someone who knows how to act and won't crumple under pressure."

"I can learn those things."

"Eva, life in the palace killed my mother. She was just like you—a commoner living a normal life. A life free to make any choice she wanted. And look how that ended. I can't do that to you. I won't do that." His choice of words cut her like a knife.

"Do you hear yourself? I'm standing here, telling you I love you, that I'll go to whatever lengths necessary to learn to be what you need to 'fit in' to palace life, and it's still not enough? Can't you see that having someone who loves you, and who you love, by your side will make you a better person? A better future king for your country? I've stood up to the media pressure just fine so far." She looked at him, her eyes imploring him to look back at her. But it seemed her last-ditch efforts were in vain.

"And today's article? I wouldn't call your reaction to that 'just fine'. I can't live like this, waiting to see if another article like that is the one that will cause us to break, to cause you to leave. It's not fair to either of us to live like that."

He may as well have cut out her heart. He didn't trust her love. He didn't believe in them. "I guess my decision from this morning to leave quietly was the right one then. I'm never going to change your mind on us. You've always had one foot out the door." She tried to keep the hurt from her voice, failing dismally.

"I've promised to marry Sophia. I'll arrange for the announcement to go out today. It should at least destroy the credibility of that ... that tabloid junk ... and prevent any ill effect on your grandfather's business. I'm sorry, Eva. I shouldn't have let it come to this."

She watched in horror as his face closed-off, as if his

crown had been invisibly placed upon his head. Eva watched him walk away, his back ramrod straight.

I'm still not good enough. Would never be good enough. No matter how much I love him with every part of my soul. He might desire her, but he didn't truly love her.

It was definitely time to go home.

15

———

The view landing into Heathrow reflected her mood. She could understand why people thought it always rained in London. The gloomy grey sky stretched endlessly, as did her heartache. A bone-deep ache had taken hold of her every limb. Every nerve throbbed with a desire to turn back time. Autopilot had clicked on. She knew, for all intents and purposes, that she was appearing as a living, breathing person. But on the inside, there was nothing. She could only hope that seeing her gramps and the familiarity of home would go some way to healing the great gaping hole that had once been her heart.

Collecting her one measly bag, she wheeled it towards the taxi area only to be brought up short by the sound of her name.

A camera flash clicked, followed shortly by shouting. Eva tensed like a rabbit caught in headlights. Please, God no, she couldn't deal with this now. Words were flung at her that she struggled to piece together.

Eva, tell us the true story. Were you really dating both princes?

Which brother is better in bed?

Which one are you in love with?

She ducked her head, using her scarf to pull it up over her hair, hiding her tear-stained cheeks. Being photographed in this state was the last straw, and she needed to hold onto some small shred of her dignity before she faced her gramps. She'd gone to Stenaco to help. Instead, she'd lost what little of her heart she'd clawed back in the past five years and screwed up any chance of fixing her gramps' business. No one would want to associate with James Tailoring after these news stories. Their reputation would be burned to the ground. At least with her gone, perhaps Gramps could hire someone new, see what could be done to salvage what was left of his dreams.

Reporters shoved microphones in her face, jostling her around in their bid to catch just one word. She could feel the fabric of her clothes dampen with sweat at the close proximity of too many ravenous journalists. Steadfastly refusing to answer, she pushed her way forward.

Relief flooded her as she spotted a taxi outside. Without checking to see if she was stealing someone else's spot she ran towards it, diving into the back seat and scooting to the far side. Never before had the stale smell of cigarettes and marked leather been so welcome.

"Twenty-two Savile Row please." She breathed what felt like her first real breath as the cabbie sped away. Her sad eyes lifted and met the cabbie's in the rear-view mirror. His old weathered face smiled back. She hoped that meant he'd be noble and not share her details to all and sundry.

The press would know where her gramps' shop was. Her personal life was in tatters, but they'd leave her alone eventually; she just had to hope the next scandal would break soon so she could rebuild her life in peace.

"I've sold the business."

Eva choked on her tea, creating a spray across her lap. She couldn't have heard him correctly.

"Pardon?" Still trying to dispel the tea, she gasped her one-word question.

"I've sold James Tailoring, to Frederick Smith. He's been showing interest in taking over this location for a few years. I've been holding off on giving him an answer, but I decided it was the right time."

Despair filled Eva to the brim. She'd thought this day couldn't get worse, but boy, was she wrong. She'd barely been home, had been working up the courage on how to broach the topic of the article with her gramps when he'd suggested they have some tea. That he had something he needed to discuss with her. She'd assumed then he'd already seen the article. Never in her wildest dreams had she imagined he'd tell her he'd sold his beloved business.

"This is all my fault." She hadn't meant to speak the words that screamed in her head, especially since they elicited such a horrified response from her Gramps.

"No, Eva dear, not your fault. I'm sorry I didn't consult you, but I knew you'd try and talk me out of the decision. I might be old, but I'm not blind, nor stupid. You changed since going to Stenaco; your voice had a lightness to it. Seeing you in the media, proudly showing off your designs and rubbing shoulders with royalty ... it suited you, Eva. I know you only went for the money, to help the business, but truth be told, I've only been holding onto this business to keep you close to me. That's my selfishness, but I realise it's been holding you back from your dreams."

She opened her mouth to deny his words, but he cut her off.

"No, don't say anything—just listen please. I sold the business, and yes, we'll have to move, but I've thought it all through and already have some places for us to look at. Places that include extra space for your workroom. This is your time to take a chance, Eva, do what you've always wanted and launch your label."

The words she'd been going to speak dried up. She couldn't deny that a small part of her sighed in relief at her gramps' words. No more tailoring boring stock-standard suits, measuring exact buttonhole stitches and angling pockets just so. Her creativity could roam free, bringing to life the designs that always danced about in her mind and on the pages of her sketchbooks. But the other part of her just felt numb. At least the tailoring had been safe; she'd known how to do that. It was risk free. Could she launch her label? Would the scandal she'd created in Stenaco ruin any chance of credibility?

The workload would be huge, something she was used to, and would help keep her mind off ... No, she couldn't even think his name. It was too painful.

Yes, she could do this. She would give it her best shot; her gramps had obviously spent a long time thinking about this decision and was making it to help her achieve her dreams. It was time to make them come true.

"Are you sure?" A small bead of excitement built as she spoke the words and saw the wide grin spread across her gramps' face. Part of her still felt in shock from this change, from what had happened in Stenaco. But this gave her something to focus on. Gave her something else she'd longed for, for a long time. It wouldn't stop her broken heart, but it eased the guilt that she'd ruined her gramps' life. He was happy, and that was enough.

"My money's on you, Eva dear. I've never been surer of anything in my life."

"Why did you let her go?" Felix swept through Henrik's door without bothering to knock, letting it slam shut behind him. Walking straight to Henrik's desk, he leant forward, closing the lid on the laptop Henrik had been working on. Surprised, Henrik snatched his fingers off the keys just before they would have been clipped within.

"Excuse me?" Henrik used his darkest tone.

"Eva. Why did you let Eva go?"

"I didn't realise stopping Eva from leaving was my decision. After all, she was your girlfriend, wasn't she? Or tailor? Or farce?"

"Don't be an idiot Henrik. You're in love with her."

The words reverberated within Henrik's head. *In love with her.* What did it matter how he felt? He'd done what was best for everyone. So why didn't he feel better? Why did it still feel like with every passing moment a new fracture appeared inside him. Wasn't a day enough time for every part of him to break?

"Henrik, are you even listening to me?" Felix's eyebrows were knitted so close together they'd formed a monobrow.

The door slamming open for a second time in as many minutes shocked both of them. Felix spun to see who'd entered. Henrik groaned at the sight of Izzie's face. It seemed both his siblings were here to give him a grilling. So much for burying himself in work.

He didn't bother standing, just raised a brow in question

towards his sister. She was the spitting image of their mother, a fact he knew their father struggled with so much it had created a rift between the two of them. The death of their mother had caused so many rifts, it was becoming a lost cause on which fragment would sink the boat.

"You let her go? What is wrong with you?" Izzie stood, arms crossed across her front, her heels adding a few inches to her short stature. Anger radiated from her every pore. Next to Felix she looked tiny, but it didn't diminish the glare she was sending his way, a fact Henrik would never utter out loud for fear of being taken apart piece by piece.

"Thank you! Someone else who sees sense. Henrik, you must go after her right his minute." Felix nodded at Izzie before returning his stare to Henrik.

Henrik wanted to laugh. Before him stood two of the most allergic people to love and commitment, lecturing him on going after a girl who they thought he'd only known for four weeks.

"I presume you're talking about Eva too, Izzie?"

"Of course, Eva. Who the heck else is there?"

"Well, you both seem to have forgotten I'm about to announce my engagement to Sophia."

"Oh phooey, you and Sophia are nothing but friends. I'd bet my Hermes' bag you haven't got the slightest bit of chemistry."

Felix jerked in reaction to Izzie's words. *Odd*, but then another thought occurred to him, one that explained a lot.

"Izzie can you give Felix and I a moment please?"

Izzie narrowed her eyes at Henrik before shifting them to Felix. "Depends. Do you promise not to throw punches whilst I'm gone?"

"I solemnly promise." He lifted his hand in a show of

honour as he spoke the words. Felix nodded but remained silent.

Henrik waited for the quiet *click* of the door before speaking his mind.

"You're in love with Sophia." It wasn't a question. It all made sense to him now. How could he not have seen this earlier? Felix's weirdness whenever Sophia was around. The fake relationship with Eva. Throwing Eva into Henrik's path constantly these past weeks ...

The fleeting look of pain coupled with a heavy expulsion of breath was all the confirmation he needed. "Love is a strong term ... I don't know I'd go so far as to say I'm in love with her. But ballpark, yes."

"Why didn't you say something to me, Felix?"

"I ... don't know. Initially I didn't take it seriously, the rumours about you two. I thought maybe you were just covering for each other. But then you told father you and Sophia had an understanding."

"Is that why you went looking for Eva?"

"She was the only woman I'd ever seen you messed up over. I knew the pressure was on you to marry, but I still questioned whether you and Sophia were serious about marrying for love or because she was helping you out. I'd never even seen you two so much as exchange a kiss."

"You've certainly been watching closely. Dammit, Felix, if you'd just said something to me?"

"What does it matter now? You love Eva. It's written all over your face. I've never seen you grimace and simultaneously smile so much as you have the past few weeks since she came back into your life. You actually look alive, like you have the ability to feel emotions. Why are you fighting that? Why are you being such a dick over a stupid deal she and I made?"

"I didn't send Eva home due to the deal, Felix. I sent her home because I can't marry her."

"Because Sophia loves you?" Felix uttered the question like each word was pushed through cement.

"No. She doesn't. Not like that. She has her own reason for needing to be married. Actually, it was her who proposed the idea. Which brings us to another problem—are you going to tell her *you* love her? I'll call off the engagement ... I can't marry her knowing you're in love with her."

Shock shone in Felix's eyes, making Henrik feel like a bastard. How far had they drifted apart that Felix thought Henrik would still marry Sophia, knowing Felix's feelings?

The door swung back inwards. Izzie marched over, determination lighting her face. "I'm back to mediate, as you're going in circles. Felix—"

"Wait, you were listening?"

"Yes! Now, Felix, to rest that pretty face of yours, Sophia won't marry Henrik knowing he's in love with Eva. She told me so herself. So, we can park your situation until later, give you time to work up the balls to tell Sophia how you feel."

"I can't believe you still listen at Henrik's door. What are you, five?"

"What are you, seven, and still mooning over Sophia?"

"Enough!" Henrik barked. A tension headache forming behind his right eyebrow. His command had stopped both Izzie and Felix in their tracks, now wearing identical sullen expressions.

"I appreciate you both trying to help. But as I've already said, I can't marry Eva. Nor Sophia, now it would seem. If you don't mind, I'd like some space to decide how I'm going to break this news to Father. He's not going to be happy with me, not that that's anything new." Henrik picked up his gold pen, enjoying the weight of it in his hand before placing it onto the closed laptop lid.

Felix grimaced before turning towards the door to Henrik's private office. Izzie sidestepped, grabbing his arm before he could take more than half a step. "Not so fast. Look, Henrik, I get it; you've had a rotten day with the story breaking. But I still don't understand why you'd walk away from love. What you and Eva have? That doesn't come along all that often ... She's put a light back in your eyes that we haven't seen since Mum died. You actually smiled at a state event. Even Father's noticed the changes in you since Eva arrived at the palace." She exchanged a quick glance with Felix before continuing. "We don't understand why you'd throw all that away?"

The slight headache now felt like a sledgehammer, banging on the inside of his skull. He should have known Izzie wouldn't just let the subject drop. He drew in a breath; air seemed to be scarce in his body at the mention of their mother. Were they right? He certainly had felt a lot of the pressure lifted from his shoulders whilst Eva was around. There was a different sort of pressure, different tension, given the situation, but underlying all the stress and worry there had been hope. And love.

Henrik picked up his pen again, looking at the few engraved words. *Henrik, with love, Mum.* It felt heavy in his palm. Its piercing coldness streaked out, just like it always did. It was one of the last things she had given him.

He never let his mind dwell on their mum, hiding the pain away in a back compartment of his mind. Along with the guilt. It seemed he could hide it there no longer. His siblings deserved the truth.

"Where to start ... you may as well sit." He waited until they'd both done so before continuing. "You know I wasn't in Australia when Mum ... well, when she took her life." He swallowed as bile rose in his throat.

"I was in Italy; that's where I met Eva. She was holidaying with some friends. I'd been struggling with the pressure Father was placing on me to give up my job, to take on more responsibility with the crown. Mum was my sounding board, and she offered a compromise. I'd quit if Father let me take some time to go away, go anywhere I wanted and just pretend I was normal. No bodyguards. Father wasn't happy, but Mum sold it to him. I wonder now if it served her purpose as much as mine. To get me away."

The faces before him were grim—he couldn't look at them anymore. Instead he found himself staring at the rose garden that lay beyond his window. The sky was crystal blue, dotted with the occasional lace wisp of cloud. The sun beamed, making the green leaves pop with colour, the lilac gate a shining invitation. It didn't seem fair that outside was sunny and beautiful, yet inside was just filled with darkness and pain.

"Two nights before I was due to fly home, I missed a call from Mum. She'd left a message, which I didn't check until I was on the flight home after I received the call from Father. She hinted at what she was going to do. If I'd just taken her call, or listened to her message earlier, instead of being caught up in my freedom with Eva, in my love, I could have prevented her death. I could have stopped her. My selfishness is to blame."

Silence met his words for a long time. So long he wasn't sure they were going to make any comments. He knew they still sat there. He could feel their glances, the blame that they must be placing on him. Feelings he'd kept well-hidden rose to the surface. Self-loathing was a poor way to describe how he felt about his actions. He could have saved their mother.

He'd chosen himself, put himself first, and it had cost his country their beloved queen. Had cost his siblings their mother, cost him his most trusted and loved supporter. He knew a life without love would be best—his mother had said so herself. Choosing someone suited to the role of his wife where feelings wouldn't interfere with tough decisions? That was his only option. Even if the decision to let Eva go, again, broke his heart into a million pieces.

Felix cleared his throat loudly. "What exactly did Mum say, Henrik?"

Henrik opened his laptop. Selecting a coded audio file, he unlocked it before hitting the play button, turning the speaker up so the delicate tones of their mother's voice could be heard clearly.

"Henrik, I hope you've enjoyed your time away. I'm sorry I haven't been able to reach you this week, but I wanted to let you know how much I love you and admire the man you have become. You must remember your path is a hard one, but I have every confidence you'll thrive in the role you were born into. Just remember, choose a wife fit for the role; the pressures of palace life are too much for someone not born into this life. I love you and will miss you, Mum."

A soft sob sounded from Izzie's direction. Tears burning the backs of his own eyes, yet he still lacked the courage to look directly at his siblings. They knew the truth now—that he could have done something to prevent his mother's suicide. If he'd just listened to his damn phone instead of trying to prove he could be independent. His need to escape and be free of the crown had cost him dearly.

"Henrik, you aren't to blame for Mum killing herself."

Felix's words were a shock. Henrik hadn't been expecting support from his direction.

"But you heard the message—"

Felix held up a hand, interrupting Henrik. "Yes, I heard the message. Maybe if you'd listened to it straight away you could have spoken to Mum, but I doubt she'd have changed her mind."

Uncertainty shone on Felix's face. It was a rare sight. Felix never looked unsure, which gave Henrik pause.

"I promised Father I wouldn't share this after I stumbled upon the information, but I don't agree that it should have been kept from you both. Mum was clinically diagnosed with depression. She'd suffered it her whole life. She'd been on medication, but about a month before she took her life, she stopped taking it. Father didn't find out until afterwards.

There isn't anything you could have done, Henrik; she'd made her decision. If you'd come home early, spoken to someone, any path I'm sure you've already gone through a million times in your head, I don't see how it would have mattered. I've had all the same thoughts. She made her choice, and from what I've read about depression and suicide, she'd have found a way no matter what. You can't shoulder all the blame for that."

Henrik felt sick. Depression was a theory he'd briefly toyed with but had resisted attributing to their mother. She'd always had a smile and kind words ready for anyone who met her. He'd just blamed the media, and himself, needing a concrete reason. But deep-down hadn't he already known Felix's revelation was the truth. What else, really, could explain his mum reaching a point where she had to take her own life?

He needed to think, to take time to sort through Felix's words. Was it really possible that it wouldn't have mattered what he'd said? Was their mother that desperate to escape this life that she'd have done so even if he'd spoken to her that night?

Her words were something Henrik had always carried in his mind, but knowing they were spoken due to such an illness changed their meaning.

"Thank you for telling us, Felix. But that doesn't change the fact I'd be locking Eva into a life of duty, of no freedom, a life where she'd have to give up her dreams."

"Henrik, do you hear yourself? Do you really think that if you love each other it would feel like a life of duty? Yes, it would be more public than most relationships, but you'd be together. Mum wouldn't want you to shut down your chance at true happiness because you were afraid. Eva is a strong woman; did you even ask her what she wants? How do you know she wouldn't give up all those things you've listed for a chance to be with you? The man she loves?" Izzie's words were quiet, but with an inner strength.

He hadn't really listened to Eva. She'd offered to learn, to do what it took, and he'd shut her out. He'd let fear put him right where he didn't want to be—the fear of loving and loosing again, which he'd done anyway. He was using his position as an excuse to shield himself from having to try. He'd surrounded himself with guilt and convinced himself Eva was better off without him.

He was an utter fool.

He would never stop missing their mother, but perhaps he could try and forgive himself for not being there. Stop the blame he placed on himself. Perhaps it was time he stopped hiding behind guilt and the crown and accept that life just had to be lived.

Would she allow him a chance to explain, this time with the whole truth, with nothing held back? It was time he opened himself up to her, put everything on the table, and did what it took to prove he was worthy of her love.

Right now, Eva was miles away, having to deal with a media circus all by herself. So much for him being a prince. He was acting more like the evil stepmother, allowing her to deal with the problems alone. But how to fix it? If he went running after her now, would she ever believe him? Would he just pour fuel onto the flames of the media lies?

He needed a plan to fix this, but how?

16

The silk sat wrapped in its plastic, unmoving from where Eva had dumped it yesterday. Who was she kidding? She'd barely achieved anything today. The first few weeks had been a whirlwind, hiding from the press and gathering all the information she needed to launch Eva James Designs.

This sort of work used to bring her joy and excitement, but of late, even designing wasn't bringing a smile to her face. The work was just a necessity. To keep busy, to keep her mind on something, anything other than repeat memories of Henrik. Of him telling her he'd made a mistake. That he would announce his engagement to stop the rumours of the love triangle. Eva had never had the courage to look for the announcement. Had actively avoided all newspapers, magazines. The internet. Anything that would throw in her face what she'd had momentarily ... then lost.

No, now was not the time to get stuck in those thoughts, again.

She'd sketched till all hours, sewn what felt like a

million samples, but it was worth the hard work. She now had a small collection she was happy with that she could show potential buyers. The silk sitting on the bolt was the last piece she needed to make up, but the message from her gramps had caused havoc on her ability to function today, to do anything.

Sophia was in London and was coming to call on Eva. She was nervous, unprepared for such a visit, her anxiety about the state of her workshop and her frazzled appearance only slightly abated by the departure of the press from her doorstep.

Guilt was a big factor as to why Eva was nervous. Sophia had been lovely to Eva, and she'd gone and slept with her soon-to-be fiancée.

It had been three weeks and two days since she'd last seen him. Not that she was counting. Well, not much. She'd stopped counting the hours, so that had to be considered progress, right?

Her groan sounded into the silence. Music—that was what she needed. Something to distract her thoughts. After flicking through her phone, she selected a moody acoustic playlist. The soft beat and crooning were enough to distract her thoughts so she could get the fabric cut. A knock at the front door had her pricking her finger on a pin. "Dammit!"

Hazard of the job. Sucking on her finger, she grabbed a Band-Aid from her stash, wrapping it around her finger before opening the door and mentally wincing at how she must look compared to the stylish, put-together woman smiling at her.

"Eva! It's great to see you." Sophia stepped forward, kissing her cheek before pulling her in for a hug. Eva was surprised by the hug, and jealous of the cloud of Dior that swamped her. Had she even put deodorant on that morning?

"Come in." Eva offered a tight smile, trying her best to keep her gaze from wandering to Sophia's left hand. Should she say congratulations? Her heart thudded and she put the emptiness in her stomach down to lack of food.

"Sorry the place is a bit of a mess. I'm putting together my first collection. Just finishing the last of the samples, but I've got an appointment with Eleanor Hayworth and—"

"Eva, you're rambling, and you won't look at me. What's going on?" Confusion laced Sophia's words and Eva broke. Tears fell down her cheeks.

"Oh, honey, come here." Sophia's arms wrapping around her only caused more tears to fall. What was wrong with her? "Is this about Henrik?"

Sophia's question evoked even more waterworks. It was like a dam had broken and just wouldn't stop. She thought she was all cried out but clearly that wasn't the case.

"You must hate me." Her sobbing made the words sound muffled, and she had to wonder if Sophia had even heard her.

"Eva, Henrik and I aren't lovers; we aren't in love. We've never even kissed. He was helping me out with something, that's all. I love him like a brother. The media turned it into some big love affair and that suited both of us."

Eva was flooded with relief. She still deemed herself a terrible friend, but a lot of her nerves dissipated.

She glanced at Sophia's hands—no ring in sight. But did that mean Henrik hadn't made the engagement announcement or that they just hadn't got a ring yet? She longed to ask Sophia for further clarification but what was the point? Even if they weren't in love, Henrik had told Eva he needed to marry someone fit for the role. And that person still wasn't her.

"Eva, I'm not going to pretend I don't know the full details. Izzie filled me in on everything I hadn't already gleaned. You're still in love with Henrik, aren't you?"

"It doesn't matter—I'm not what he needs. He told me to go, that I'm not royal material."

Sophia just looked at her, shaking her head. "Look, come to Stenaco with me. That's actually why I'm here—to convince you to come back and finish Izzie's dress."

Now Eva felt like an idiot. Sophia was a messenger for Izzie, and she'd bawled all over her. "I can't go back. Besides the obvious reason, the media will have a field day if I return to Stenaco."

"Well, I for one know the article that was printed was a load of rubbish. Papers are always spinning information to suit their own needs. Besides, didn't you read the retraction article? Let's put something new into the media—loads of images of your wonderful gown on royalty. It'll do wonders for your label launch. Which I'm so excited about, by the way."

"Wait, what retraction article?"

"Come with me and I'll show you on the plane."

"No Sophia, I can't ... even if there was a retraction printed ... I don't want to see him. I can't. The hurt is too raw still."

"Then come back to spend time with your friends, Izzie and I miss you. I promise we can keep it secret—private planes, royal favours, no need to see anyone you don't want to. Please? This is your big moment. It's only fitting you're there in person to see your first couture piece hit centre stage."

Eva had to admit she longed to see Izzie in the gown she'd laboured over. See it in person. She'd question why she agreed to this later, but now she just wanted to spend time with friends. It was only one night, her business launch would still be there tomorrow.

Eva held her breath as she took her first step back into the palace. It was just a simple trip to finish off Izzie's dress and then leave. For good this time.

She let her breath out in a whoosh, taking in the opulence. Had she really thought she'd belonged here? For that one night she had, but seeing it now, she knew she'd been wrong.

"Eva! Thank God you came!" The enthusiastic greeting nearly bowled her over, and knocked all negative thoughts clear out of her head. It was impossible to feel anything but happiness around Izzie; she was such a bundle of energy.

Eva returned her embrace, holding on tight. Her heart took a pang, one of many she'd experienced since stepping back on Stenish soil. She'd missed Izzie, Sophia, and Felix, and ... no, she wouldn't let her heart lead her there. She'd locked the key on those feelings. Professionalism—that was what she needed to focus on.

Stepping back, she smiled as bright a smile as she could muster before letting herself be led off towards the fit room. The bucket of chilled French champagne didn't surprise her, though the count of five crystal gleaming glasses did. Surely Henrik wasn't coming to the fitting? Please no ... that would be too cruel, surely her friend wouldn't disrespect her wishes like that? Her nerves from earlier came back in force.

She'd agreed to come back, but only if she didn't have to see Henrik. Those were her terms.

Izzie chattered, filling Eva in on idle news about the palace and events she'd been to, what people had worn. How excited she was about Eva's decision to start her label. Eva offered polite nods or slight smiles, still distracted by the count of glasses. It didn't take long to lose herself in her work though. The dress was exquisite, by far the best work Eva had ever done. Its pleated bodice fit snug against Izzie's slight frame, the tiny waist flaring into full skirts. The embroidery on the underside floated and danced as Izzie moved, appearing as if she walked through flowers. The hand hemming wasn't quick, but Izzie seemed happy to stand on the dais and chatter whilst Eva worked her way around.

Finally, it was done. Eva snipped off the last thread. She stood back, taking stock of her work. She hoped Izzie was happy with the outfit. Surely it would win her best dressed status in the magazines over Harriet.

"I. Love. It! I think it's the prettiest thing I've ever worn. Seriously, Eva, you are crazy talented." Izzie launched herself at Eva, attempting to clasp her into a close hug but the layers of tulle and silk had other ideas, leaving the two giggling.

The *click* of the door had Eva swinging towards it. She whooshed out her breath as Felix and Sophia walked through in their evening finery. Felix offered a hesitant smile before coming over and offering a hug of his own. Eva hadn't been sure what type of reception she'd receive from him since she'd left without so much as a goodbye. It was nice to see them all together, but it brought back an ache so great that Eva just wanted to escape before it splintered her in two.

"Good to see you again, Felix. I'm all finished, so I'm going to head back to the airport if that's okay?"

"Actually, no, it's not." Felix looked at Izzie and received a nod. "We want you to stay for the ball. No, don't say anything yet—please, just this one last thing. Besides, you owe me—you never finished your last week as my pretend girlfriend."

Eva had tried to interrupt but stopped at Felix's words. Part of her desperately wanted to attend the ball tonight, to see Izzie wearing her dress centre stage, but she couldn't take the risk. She racked her brains for an excuse.

"I have nothing appropriate to wear to a ball. Thank you, but really, I should just get going ..." Her words drifted as a mannequin was wheeled in. On it was a full-length gown in blue silk. Fabric dipped from the middle, sweeping across the shoulders. The fitted bodice was drawn in, a dainty jewelled belt at the waist. The skirt of the dress looked to be made of many layers, the top with slits, which Eva knew would float when walked in.

The design was quite simple. She'd know, since it was one of hers.

It was one of the first in her sketch book from years ago. From ... "Where did ... I don't understand how ..." Her stilted words sounded stupid to her ears, but the disconnect between brain and mouth was too great.

"Your gramps sent us a picture and your measurements. Do you like it?"

Eva was sure her imitation of a goldfish was spectacular. She wasn't even sure who had spoken, their words a hazy whisper permeating the fog that surrounded her brain. Finally, she worked through the words that were sticking and looked away from the gown to the hopeful faces that surrounded her.

"Of course I like it … I love it. It's one of my most favourite designs. Seeing it come to life is, well … magical. But why would you do this for me?"

"No time for questions. Just get dressed." Izzie quipped, then started pushing Felix out the door, ordering him to find elsewhere to loiter before the ball.

Both Izzie and Sophia were dressed, looking elegant and regal. Eva knew the dress fit the bill but wasn't so sure her wearing it would. Mentally shrugging, she squared her shoulders and knew it was time to just go with the flow.

She'd been honest when she told Sophia she wasn't ready to see Henrik. But being here now? Well, she was clearly just a glutton for punishment.

Izzie popped the cork on the bottle of champagne, sending it flying into the high ceilings with an excited yelp. Eva accepted a glass of the fizzing bubbles from Sophia. Her eyes flicked in surprise at Sophia's next words.

"To fairy-tale endings, and all of us finding our very own princes." Sophia's eyes held Eva's as she spoke, like her words were directed at Eva.

"C'mon, let's get you washed, primped and dressed. Don't want to keep everyone waiting."

There was no time to dwell on Sophia's strange toast or Izzie's odd behaviour, particularly her insisting on Eva wearing crown jewels. If her stomach lit with butterflies and excitement, she pushed it aside, focusing on how she was going to walk in the sky-high satin heels Izzie had pushed into her hands to finish the outfit. She was very much a mid-height heel-wearer, so she hoped it wouldn't show. She particularly hoped she wouldn't embarrass herself by falling down the stairs which led to the ballroom in the palace. Maybe that's why Cinderella ran off without her shoe, the darn thing probably fell off…

The dress fitted to perfection, the way it clung to her skin but wasn't so tight she couldn't breathe. Whoever had made it had done a beautiful job; she had to admire their skill in bringing her design to life. Searching the room for a mirror to check she looked okay, she spotted one in the corner.

"Nope! No time for that. Take it on good authority you look amazing. C'mon." Izzie and Sophia took an arm each, marching her out of the room. Their behaviour really was very strange.

"But ..." Eva could feel the jewelled necklace against her neck, its cool presence somehow calming. Lifting a hand, she fingered the floral design, inset with what she could only assume were sapphires. The design was strangely similar to the patterns on her beaded bracelet. Her bracelet that Henrik had given her all those years ago. Glancing down, she checked its presence at her wrist. She was so used to its light weight there she often had to check.

"Actually, Eva, I just remembered something I have to show Sophia. We'll meet you in the ballroom."

Huh? Was she kidding? Eva didn't want to go to a ball she wasn't even invited to and arrive by herself! Particularly as she hadn't wanted to go in the first place. She opened her mouth to say as much but Izzie and Sophia were already dashing off back the way they'd come from, their skirts floating out behind them.

Now, Eva was seriously confused. Maybe she should wait?

The stairs lay just before her. She knew they led down to the foyer just outside the ballroom. She could hang back up here until Sophia and Izzie returned ... but that would be cowardly. If she was going to attend, she really needed to grow some backbone. Perhaps it would be better to be able to slip in unnoticed, a feat easier to achieve if she was alone.

Her foot wobbled slightly on the first step, but with each step she felt a deeper sense of calm, of strength. She could do this, could set aside her feelings and just try and make the most of being here. Izzie had promised to ensure her dress got a lot of press coverage so that had to make coming worthwhile. Perhaps being photographed there, as the designer, would help quash all the silly rumours about her being in love with both princes and she could just start over. Sophia had showed her the retraction article, which had gone to print the day after she'd arrived home in London, but it hadn't deterred the London press these past few weeks, so she doubted it fooled anyone else either.

Focus on her career.

That was what she'd been doing the past five years—why ruin a good thing? She'd made peace over her guilt about Gramps' business, and really, she'd never seen him so happy and relaxed now that he was retired. He had loved helping set up her label and was a wealth of knowledge.

Her thoughts had drifted so far, she didn't notice the lack of people in the foyer, or the gentle music that sere-naded the room as she took her first step through the ball-room doors. Her heels echoed, a slight clip with each slowly taken step. Goosebumps spread along her arms. Her heart started to beat faster. Swallowing the dryness in her mouth she found herself robbed of speech. The room was decked out with a sea of dusky pink flowers. Tiny fairy lights glit-tered within the garlands. The lights were dimmed, the evening glow lighting the room, highlighting the lone man who stood on the balcony.

He turned at the sound of her gasp. No man should be allowed to look that good. He'd looked so royal dressed in his official dress whites at the state ball a few weeks ago, but tonight he wore a tuxedo. Classic black, with a sapphire blue pocket square, matching her dress to perfection. Like it was made to.

Her fingers flew to the necklace, too afraid to put together the dots before her, to hope for what her heart desired more than anything.

Flawless. That was his first thought. She looked absolutely flawless. He gulped at the nerves that engulfed his thoughts. Eva was here. He'd taken his time orchestrating just this moment. He'd better not stuff this up. More than his heart was at stake.

He let his eyes take in everything: her hair swept into a loose bun, held in place by a delicate tiara. The gentle curve of her neck and shoulders, the fabric sweeping away, beautiful lines to show off the necklace he'd had designed especially for her. It would be her first crown jewel, or so he hoped, with many more to come. He just had to convince her to take the position. To take him. To accept his heart.

She'd stopped in the centre of the ballroom, surrounded by powerful floral scents, the glittering of lights in the backdrop making her appear even more like an illusion. Up to this moment, until she was standing there in front of him, he hadn't been sure she'd come. Couldn't be sure his siblings and Sophia would pull off such a miracle.

"You came." His voice was husky, the words whispered with reverence. His shoes clipped and echoed on the tiles, just as hers had a moment ago. He heard the music he'd carefully selected, requested to be played the moment she appeared through the double doors. Crooning words that spoke of love lost and then found. He hoped it would act as an omen to their story.

"Eva you look ... breath-taking."

Slight pink, the same colour as the roses about the room, tinged her cheeks. Her eyes flirted with his only to go back to studying her fingernails. He barely caught her whispered "thank you".

He took a step closer so he stood before her, close enough to capture her fingers in both of his palms, stopping her avoidance in its tracks. Close enough to feel drunk on the scent of her, her unique floral essence more powerful than the room full of roses.

"I need to apologise." He dipped at the knees to bring their faces into line until her eyes met his. Looking into the golden brown of her irises brought a smile to his features. He'd always found her eyes irresistible. From that first moment she'd tripped into his arms in Italy, he should have known then she was it for him. His love for her had always been that strong; he'd just been too stupid and allowed other factors get in the way.

"Come outside. There are things I need to say."

"Henrik, did you orchestrate this? Is this why I'm here? For you to apologise?"

"Yes. I asked Felix and Izzie to help get you here. And Sophia—it was her suggestion to come see you in London."

"Henrik, I don't need an apology. It's fine. We're good." She hurried the words out, glancing about the room, searching for something. "We shouldn't be in here alone. What if someone takes pictures again? I think there are enough rumours about us. I don't want to cause further issues for you."

Eva spun on her heel, but Henrik stilled her with a hand on her arm. "Wait, Eva. Sophia and I aren't engaged. We aren't getting married. We don't love each other, not that way. Sophia has to get married to inherit some money from an estranged aunt. It's complicated, but it was a mutually beneficial agreement. Until I saw you again. Then it wasn't beneficial anymore."

He felt the confusion in her eyes like a hit to the solar plexus. He'd caused this hurt, this worry. He could only hope she'd let him make it up to her.

"Why?"

"Because I couldn't pretend anymore. I couldn't pretend I didn't still love you with every fibre in my being. As much as I've tried to fight it, it's always been you, Eva."

Concern flitted through Henrik as tears appeared in Eva's eyes, their watery trail slipping down her cheeks. Her sniff was quickly followed by a smile more brilliant than anything he'd ever seen before. "You mean it? You love me?"

"Yes! That's what I'm trying to explain here. This isn't quite how I was hoping to tell you. I'd planned to get you outside, into a hopefully romantic moonlit evening, where I could explain everything. How much of a fool I've been. Then tell you how much I love you, with everything I have. And convince you to be my wife, my princess." With that, he dropped to one knee, watching delight dance across her face as more happy tears followed those from a moment ago. Using the hand that wasn't gripping her fingers, he fished out a ruby-red velvet box, flicking it open. He'd practiced that move in the mirror, with the thought he wanted to be holding at least one of the hands of the woman he loved when he asked her this most important question.

"Eva James, will you do me the honour of becoming my wife? My equal, my princess and one day, my queen? I know it's a lot to ask. I come with baggage, and God knows we won't have a private life like most. But if you can forgive me, I promise to be there, loving you, every step of the way."

Eva swallowed, staring at the ring in his hand. Some of the sparkle that had been shining so brightly dulled before she shook her head.

Henrik felt the movement like a punch in the gut.

She knelt on the ground before him. "No. I want to say yes, with every part of me I want to say yes. But you ordered me away. In Italy, you never showed up. Now I understand why, but if you'd loved me, you could have at least sent a note. Last month, you kissed me, made love to me, then pushed me to leave. Told me you were going to marry Sophia. Now you've brought me back ... you're telling me you love me." She shook her head slowly, tears continuing to run down her cheeks. "How can I trust you won't change your mind again?" Her hand slipped from his to lay in her lap. Every word she spoke was true; he'd acted in such an ungentlemanly manner. He was ashamed. Knew his mother would be ashamed.

"You're right. I owe you an explanation. But before I start, take this." He handed the ring box to her. She held it hesitantly, as if it were a loaded gun. "Once I'm finished, you can decide."

Taking a deep breath, he repositioned himself on the floor, his arm slung across his knee, his other leg bent beneath. They must look a sight, sitting on the empty ball-room floor, clad in finery.

"That night I didn't show up in Italy, I'd planned to tell you everything. That I was royalty, to invite you to Stenaco. I wanted you to meet my mother. She had always been my biggest advocate, my emotional support. She understood my path was more difficult than Felix's or Izzie's. That our father always expected me to be twice as good. That night when I received the call she was dying, my thoughts just scattered. I'd fought so hard to have that week's escape; I felt guilty that I wasn't home. Then when I arrived, and she was already gone ... I found a voicemail from her and have since blamed myself for not preventing her death."

"Oh, Henrik ... you can't put that on yourself."

"I know that now. I told Felix and Izzie. I played them the voicemail. A reminder I've always kept. Felix told me our mother suffered from depression, something I wasn't aware of. Or hadn't wanted to see. She was *my* pillar of strength. I've thought about it a lot over the last few weeks though, and there are memories ... times when it was clear she wasn't happy in her life here. That she was struggling. I just hadn't wanted to see it."

Eva took his hand, shifting to be closer to him. Her closeness brought comfort.

"After listening to the voicemail, I decided I didn't deserve love. That my life, my path, would be better without it. It hurt too much. My father loved my mother. Seeing how shattered, how broken he was ..." He took a ragged breath, fixing his eyes on hers. "I had your details, Eva. I knew where you lived. But I turned my back on our feelings, convinced myself I was doing you a favour in letting you go."

Her eyes flittered away from his, down to the ring cradled in her hand, biting her bottom lip. He worried his words would hurt her, but he needed to tell her the truth.

"I tried to forget you. The press started in on how I never seemed to date anyone, questioning whether I'd ever get married. The opinion and support of the royal family was low. I hated the media after what they'd put the family through after Mum's death. I just wanted to fix the situation, prove my worth by marrying Sophia and getting our family back on track. We'd both been stalling over making any sort of formal announcement when I came to London. Then I walked into your atelier and lost my heart all over again. Thanks to Felix."

"Felix?" Eva's eyebrows knitted in confusion

"Felix wanted you back on the scene. So, he tracked you down. He knew I'd fallen for you in Italy. It seemed he sensed I'd never gotten over you."

"Felix set me up ..."

"I tried to stay away, Eva. I bought into the idea that you were dating my brother, but I think part of me knew it was always a ruse, that Felix had an ulterior motive. I tried to fight my feelings, but you fit in so well, like you were born to palace life. You handled Harriet, who is a seasoned professional antagonist. You didn't flinch in front of the media, at any of the royal events. You didn't mind when I took you to the markets and I was stopped by every single person. You just looked so happy, and natural. You brought back a lightness I hadn't known, that I'd buried with my mother."

"If that was the case, why did you send me away?"

"Seeing your face when I handed you that article. You crumpled. And instead of being there for you, I shut down. I let all my insecurities get in the way. Instead of seeing the true reason for your upset—the impact on your gramps' business—I saw you falling apart from the pressure of palace life. Like Mum had warned against. I'd been hiding my heart behind this hurt for so long, it was like I'd been waiting for this exact situation to happen. I used it as a shield. I used the supposed announcement of the engagement to make you go home. I thought I was doing the right thing for both of us. I didn't want you to suffer the same fate as my mother. But, like before, I was wrong. I've been miserable. I can't forget you, Eva, not again, not unless you tell me you're done with me. And even then, I'll keep trying to win you back. I love you."

"You acted like a jerk. Twice. You hurt me, Henrik." He felt her eyes roving across his face, the distress clear.

"I know, and I hate myself for that. But I promise to try every day to make it up to you. To show you I have changed. I'm ready to believe in our love. It makes me a better person. Eva, you make me a better person. Please tell me what I can do to make you give me another chance?"

She fingered the ring, slipping it out of its case, before putting it back in. She searched his eyes, looking for what, he didn't know. He could only hope more than anything that she'd find it. In him.

Her voice was quiet, almost a whisper. "Tell me you love me."

"I love you. I love you a thousand times over. I have never loved anyone the way I love you, and even if you say no and walk out on me, I will never love anyone as much as I do you." His eyes pleaded with hers, his breath bated as he steeled himself for her answer.

"Then ... yes. My answer is yes."

A loud yelp of joy sounded about the room before he realised it was him. Clapping sounded from the doorway, and he gathered they weren't alone, but he didn't care. She'd healed him and was giving him the chance of a lifetime—to shower her in his love.

"Eva, I love you." The words were whispered against her lips before he kissed her. The feel of her soft skin under his hands as he cupped her face felt like coming home.

***

Eva watched as her fiancé danced with an elderly woman

decked out in a lavender gown, dripping with enough jewels that Eva worried she'd topple over if left standing alone. She couldn't wipe the smile from her face. Henrik's explanation had allowed the last piece of her heart to tumble. Nerves had sprung at the idea of being a future royal, but she shoved them aside. Tomorrow would be soon enough to worry about that, and she knew with Henrik by her side, she'd be just fine.

She couldn't wait to call her gramps and tell him the happy news. Hopefully she could talk him into moving to Geravia. She certainly planned to throw everything at the offer so he couldn't possibly refuse.

"That's some rock you got there. I knew kissing you felt like kissing a sister." Felix laughed at his own humour.

Eva thumped a hand to his chest. "Don't jest; you're stuck with me now. And I happen to know you had a hand in this, so let me just say ... thank you." She leaned in to give him a quick hug which was interrupted by a loud cough.

"I leave you alone for five seconds and you're hugging my brother?"

Eva thumped Henrik just as she'd done Felix. His grunt was satisfying.

"Too soon to joke?" he asked.

"Yep, your time is better spent showing me you love me. You're not off the hook for all you put me through just yet."

Henrik's eyes glittered with love and with something else. Cheekiness, she realised, as he swept her up into his arms and spun her around in a circle. She linked her hands behind his neck, anchoring herself as he carried her out of the ballroom, onto the terrace. He slid her slowly to the ground, keeping close contact on purpose if the wicked glint in his eyes was anything to go on.

"Eva ..."

"Henrik?"

"I told you to be careful."

His words made her laugh, lightness and love filling every part of her. That one word had started it all, but she knew now she'd never have to be careful around Henrik.

He was her everything and always would be.

The End

ABOUT THE AUTHOR

Jayne Kingsley writes contemporary romance filled with fashionable and fun heroines and the hunky heroes that capture their hearts. She currently resides on the picturesque south coast of NSW with her two young daughters and her own real-life gorgeous hero.

www.jaynekingsley.com

facebook.com/jaynekingsleyauthor

instagram.com/jaynekingsleyauthor

bookbub.com/authors/jaynekingsleyauthor

PREVIEW OF BOOK 2 HER CONVENIENT PLAYBOY PRINCE

Read on for a sneak peek of *'Her Convenient Playboy Prince: The Stenish Royals Book 2'*

CHAPTER 1

*L*ady Sophia placed a sparkly heel onto the red velvet carpet that ran the length of the aisle. *First step done.* She could do this, really it wasn't so bad. If you ignored the fact this was being nationally televised and that three months ago she was meant to be the bride in this event—not the maid of honour—then it was fine. Of course not an ounce of this momentary nervousness showed on her face, she was a consummate professional. Years of training and hiding her personal feelings stood her in good stead. She could thank her mum for that at least, though not much else.

A hush swept over the room, leaving Sophia with no doubt that Eva had taken her place behind her. Sophia knew that Eva looked every inch a princess to be, anyone in the crowd not looking at her had to be completely daft. Sophia had to fight the urge to turn and look at her new friend. They'd only known each other a few short months but no one could be a more perfect match for her long time friend.

A quick glance at Crown Prince Henrik, who stood at

the front of the cathedral, confirmed her guess. His eyes were glued over her shoulder, his mouth turned up in delight, his eyes pools of love. She couldn't stop the happiness that bloomed in her heart at seeing Henrik so happy. He and Eva were made for each other and regardless of what the tabloids had printed about Sophia supposedly being destitute and devastated, she couldn't be happier for her friends.

It did however, place a slight dent in her plans to get married. Her stomach did a little flip but she ignored it. *That's a problem for another day.* Today was about Henrik and Eva and their wedding that was a long time coming. Once she heard back from the private investigator about her Aunt, she could go back to worrying about her lack of upcoming nuptials and what the devil she'd do about her mother.

Taking the last step that brought her to the left of the alter, she joined Princess Isabella—better known as Izzie—and delicately spun to stand across from Henrik and his brother, Felix, who were resplendent in their royal uniforms. She tried to avoid looking at Prince Felix but failed dismally, her eyes seeking his face without permission.

Oh.

Slate blue clashed back at her, a smirk hovering around his mouth. He winked at her and against her better judgement Sophia felt a treble of excitement course through her. Felix had always made something insider her shiver, a fact she'd certainly never share with anyone. For one thing, his list of conquests could stretch the Pacific Ocean, twice, and she had no time to join that queue. A dalliance of any kind didn't appeal to her right now. What she needed was a husband, preferably one who'd agree to marry her and then leave her the heck alone.

After a lifetime of being bossed around and dressed up

like a barbie doll, some alone time and freedom to just life her life however she wanted sounded like heaven.

Swallowing back nerves, Sophia flicked her gaze back to Eva who had reached the alter. The other woman's dress was an art form. Layer after layer of silk glistened with three dimensional embroidered roses, wisteria and butterflies. The bodice was fitted, the skirts flaring out in a true ballgown style. Whisper fine tulle covered her arms, edged with tiny beads. Sophia new fashion and this was right up there with the haute couture designs she watched each year at the Paris and Milan showings. She accepted the cascade of white roses, babies breath and mauve wisteria, the green ivy catching on the silk skirt of her own gown. She doubted if Eva would have noticed if the whole bouquet had fallen to the ground or burst into flames. Her and Henrik were locked in their own bubble that felt like it could set off fireworks.

The words spoken by the priest brought a hush to the gathering, but it was the words spoken by Eva and Henrik themselves that brought tears to even the most cold hearted in the room. Sophia could feel moisture brewing in her own eyes and blinked away the emotion. Love wouldn't be something she'd chose in her future. She'd seen first hand how damaging that emotion could be—but deep down she knew that Henrik and Eva would be an exception—their love would last a lifetime.

They sealed their words with a kiss, Eva's tiara glittered with diamonds that couldn't match the euphoria that shone on her face. Which was saying something.

Sophia followed the newlyweds towards an anti-room where they would sign the marriage certificate and other legal documents. Felix fell into step beside her. He silently held out a handkerchief, his initials embroidered in neat maroon script along one edge.

"Thank you," Sophia murmured, accepting the piece of cloth to dab at her eyes.

"So do you feel like you've dodged a bullet? You know, since Henrik is desperately in love with someone else." Felix' tone suggested he was aiming for flippant but he had a funny look on his face.

If she didn't know better she'd call it nervousness but it was so odd to see anything other than his cocky assuredness that she dismissed her thought. "I'm not sure if you're trying to be funny or serious or if you're falling dismally somewhere in between."

"Yeah. Sorry. Weddings make me nervous." He tugged at the high neck of his royal uniform.

"Now that I can easily believe." She arched a brow, amusement laced her words.

"Though for the right woman I'm sure I could change my tune." There was that look again.

"Ha! Likely story Felix. Given you've sampled most of the eligible women under forty and possibly more besides, I would say you're not about to change your tune as you put it." She threw him a sideways smile and was surprised to see his brows creased slightly. He caught her eye, the frown smoothing immediately.

"What can I say, I like women. And they like me."

Now there was the Felix she knew. And the very reason she would never entertain any serious thoughts about him, even if her body begged her too on any occasion that brought them into close proximity. *And other times.* She shooed the unwelcome thought away. Prince Felix was absolutely the last man she'd consider getting involved with. Not that he'd offered, and nor could she be bothered waiting in line, just to fall into his little black book and become another dismissed notch. *No thank you.*

He cleared his throat, the sound warranting a look from Eva.

"The romance of the wedding getting to you already hey brother dearest?" Eva's smile was impish. Considering the two had played pretend boyfriend/girlfriend not so long ago, for reasons Sophia still wasn't entirely clear on, they appeared to have moved onto being close friends. Eva had stepped into the family and brought a sense of light and sunshine back to Henrik's world. For that alone Sophia would be her friend for life. There was also the added bonus she was simply so likeable one couldn't *not* be her friend.

"No, no. Far be it from me to not enjoy an occasion that brings two loved up souls together. As well as plenty of champagne, good food, music and gloriously fine women dressed in their best. I look forward to out-dancing you."

It was Sophia's turn to sign the certificate, the others shifting to give her space. She'd felt a little odd that it had been her who'd been asked to take this honour, when Izzie —Henrik and Felix's younger sister—was also part of the wedding party but Eva had been strangely insistent. Izzie had been too.

With a flick of her wrist her signature scrawled along the dotted line. She allowed her gaze to wander to Felix's signature. It was flamboyant, yet also elegant, the combination the exact description she'd give the man himself. She felt someone move behind her a moment before Felix's head appeared close to her own. His manly scent enveloped her in a way that had her wanting to drag in breaths and hyperventilate on the smell. Not a good reaction.

"You know, you're going to have to dance with me too. I

promise I've improved since last time. No stepping on yours toes. I've had lessons."

Feigning a disinterest she certainly didn't feel, Sophia raised a brow and turned her head slightly. The move brought them even closer. Little puffs of heat spotted her cheek with each breath he took. His eyes held hers, then offered a slow seductive wink, almost daring her. To what? She didn't want to know.

Instead she stood as he also straightened, her heels bringing her into alignment with his eyes which hadn't budged from their assessment of her.

"I wouldn't want to hold you from your adoring fans. Surely there's a young lady out there you haven't taken to bed yet who'll be desperate to dance with you. Far be it from me to stand in the way of that." Her arch tone sounded a little breathless even to her ears.

She side-stepped around him, curious that his trademark grin didn't quite reach his eyes and he didn't make a return remark. Sophia moved towards Eva and Henrik, giving them both enthusiastic hugs and congratulating them once more. She was beyond happy that her longtime friend had finally come to his senses and admitted his love for Eva. The rest of the ceremony, walking down the aisle and standing for countless photographs was a blur for Sophia. Her mind had settled back on her own mounting problem. If she didn't marry soon, she'd loose a huge inheritance—from an Aunt she'd never even known about until six months ago.

Just how did Sophia reach the age of twenty eight and not have known her deranged mother had a sister?

***

Felix ordered himself to stop looking at Sophia. God he was pathetic. What was it about her that left him a muddle mouthed teen whose first crush had just smiled at him for the first time? It was lame and he hated himself for not just finding the balls to be honest with her.

But he was playing the long game here.

He didn't know why, but Sophia was the one and only woman who had always reached deep inside him and left him with feelings of wanting to settle down. Thoughts that usually brought him out in hives. But he'd dithered, unable to lock himself into any form of decision. That had been until his older brother Henrik had told him of his plans to wed Sophia.

Which would have been a huge mistake.

Henrik may not, but Felix remembered a drunken night, just days after their mothers death, when Henrik had opened up about the girl he'd met in Italy. A girl whose name was Eva. He'd professed a love so deep and pure that his words had stuck with Felix. Plus it had been the first time in a while that Felix had felt connected to his brother. Growing up as the second prince afforded him a lot of leniencies, as well as pitfalls. He'd grown up knowing Henrik would always be the number one child, their father had been sure that message had been locked in tight. What he hadn't realised was how lonely that would leave him. Feeling like there was always this invisible wall between the two brothers.

Felix tried to shake the memories, knowing that he'd done the right thing. It might have been an odd way to go about it but he'd known if he'd just marched up to his brother and told him to marry Eva not Sophia, that his brother would never have entertained the idea. Country first, no emotions allowed. No, Felix had made sure Henrik realised his folly for himself, which meant the decision rang true for his proud and straight laced brother. He'd made sure Henrik had recaptured his joy.

And he'd made sure Sophia didn't marry the wrong brother.

Of course, working out how to get her to see he'd be her perfect partner left a lot to be desired.

For one thing, Felix couldn't even trust his own feelings. He'd always been the fickle prince, the one who'd moved through women and interests like he went through socks. Could he really commit to Sophia and promise never to waiver in that promise?

His heart had been lost to her for years but could he truly say that wasn't just because he'd never allowed himself to actually pursue her? Was she just his ultimate quest?

Gah! He was a fool.

Distracted as he was he didn't realise he had company until he felt a small pinch to his ass. He cocked a brow at the curvaceous brunette he'd noticed watching him during dinner.

"You know that could be construed as harassment in many countries." He spoke lazily, hiding the annoyance he really felt at being interrupted.

She dipped her head to the side in an artful and most likely practised fashion. Her heavily made up eyes fluttered at him. "Oops. Maybe you should take me somewhere private so I can apologise."

Once upon a time he would have fallen for that. But ever since he'd witnessed his brothers fall into the depths of love he'd found himself left somewhat cold when it came to the opposite sex, Sophia the only exception to that. This overt invitation left a dusty taste in his mouth.

"Perhaps some other time. I'm on duty."

She pouted, not perturbed by his declining her obvious offer. "No one will miss us. It's not like you're still on duty. Lady Perfect appears to be leaving, so you're off the hook."

Her words had Felix spinning, catching a glimpse of Sophia's perfectly coiffed hair and elegant figure disappearing through the floral arch and out of the reception area. He moved after her, ignoring the indignant shout of his name. He was sure Miss Busy Hands would find some other willing man to entertain her whims. Right now there was only one woman Felix planned to pursue.

Sophia disappeared into the east wing entrance of the castle, leaving Felix with a sense of disappointment. He hadn't even found an opportunity to dance with her.

"For someone who went to the lengths you did, you're certainly keeping your distance."

Felix jolted, being taken by surprise again. Seriously what was with him tonight? Normally he was far more on the ball. Eva and Henrik stood arm in arm, a stance that they seem to have adopted since becoming engaged. It was almost like they worried it they let go of each other they'd be forever parted again. Felix mentally rolled his eyes at his pathetically sappy thought.

He chose to speak to Eva, whose eyes didn't glint with knowing amusement. His brother was taking enormous pleasure in Felix's unrequited feelings making him wish he'd never confided in his siblings. "There's no rush. She's not going anywhere."

"Uh ..." Eva glanced to Henrik who nodded slightly, "actually she is. We've loaned her the plane. She needs to go to Ireland."

Shock ricocheted through Felix's chest. "Ireland? What! *Why?*"

Again with the shared unsure look. What the hell weren't they telling him? "She didn't explain a lot. But she's looking for someone."

"Well then I'm sure she'd like company."

Felix jogged off before Eva or Henrik could say anything more though he heard his brother call his name.

There was no way Felix was letting Sophia go off looking for some person without letting her know of his true feelings. He'd waited long enough.

FREE ROMANTIC SHORT STORY

If you enjoyed Henrik & Eva's story and want more - sign up to my newsletter and receive a FREE short story of how they met in Italy.

Newsletter sign up: https://dl. bookfunnel.com/yx7i93qzpd